MAKING TRACK

Also by Stack Sutton
in Thorndike Large Print ®

End of the Tracks

MAKING TRACK

Stack Sutton

Thorndike Press • Thorndike, Maine

Published in 1994 by arrangement with Walker Publishing Company, Inc.

All the characters and events portrayed in this work are fictitious.

Thorndike Large Print ® Western Series.

The tree indicium is a trademark of Thorndike Press.

The text of this Large Print edition is unabridged.
Other aspects of the book may vary from the original edition.

Set in 16 pt. News Plantin by Penny Lee Picard.

Printed in the United States on acid-free, high opacity paper. ∞

Library of Congress Cataloging in Publication Data

Sutton, Stack.
 Making track / Stack Sutton.
  p. cm.
 ISBN 0-7862-0215-7 (alk. paper : lg. print)
 1. Railroad engineering — Fiction. 2. Large type books.
I. Title.
[PS3569.U898M35 1994]
813'.54—dc20   94-8815

For Kay,
who was there through thick and thin

CHAPTER 1

As the Denver Railroad's supply train ground to a halt, Creed Weatherall, the railroad's troubleshooter, dropped from the caboose. His gaze automatically ran south, following the new track, which ran ten miles in that direction. If General Sheffield, head of the Denver line, had his way that track would one day reach Mexico City. But there was competition from the Colorado Railroad, run by Don Adams, and after what Weatherall had heard in Pueblo, he wondered if the general's dream was about to hit a snag.

Weatherall glanced left toward the Colorado camp and its set of tracks paralleling the Denver line. The two railroads had been in a race ever since leaving Denver to see who could first reach Raton Pass, astride the Colorado–New Mexico border. So far they'd matched each other rail for rail, spike for spike, with some dirty tricks thrown in between. Weatherall had heard that Dallas Mason had been hired as the Colorado's troubleshooter, and that meant things were about to heat up even more.

The Denver camp was situated about a hundred miles east of Pueblo, Colorado. Near it, the Arkansas River gurgled on its eastern flow. They camped here instead of ten miles farther south where the track ended, because water was scarce there. It was easier to take the work train out every morning and back every evening.

Weatherall surveyed the dirt street, which fronted an array of tents and wooden shacks. What he saw looked like any other "hell on wheels" town, a hastily thrown together enterprise that followed the railroad. The town's biggest attraction was Bullard's Emporium, and it occupied the street's far end. The Emporium was nothing more than a huge tent with a fancy name, but its liquor, gambling, and women were the best in camp.

This was a hard camp. Harder than any Weatherall had encountered when he had worked the Central Pacific. Hardly a night passed without some kind of ruckus, and muggings were so frequent as to go unnoticed. Weatherall didn't like the town or what it stood for, but it had a purpose. Hardworking men far from their families needed a place to blow off steam. These tents and shacks provided that place.

Weatherall hoofed down track until he

cleared the supply engine. It was too early for his wife to be back from her mail run, so he would have time to see Colonel Thompson, the Denver's chief engineer, and wash the dust from his throat before she got home. He'd missed Charlotte. They'd been married three years, but it seemed like only yesterday that he'd met her. Looking back, he wondered how he had survived for twenty-seven years without her. She was his life now.

One big hand fumbled at his vest pocket and lifted an American Horologe. He snapped the cover open. In a couple of hours, this empty street would be full of life. After repocketing the watch, he hiked over the track and turned north toward the spur line that held the colonel's coach, followed by Weatherall's coach and three supply coaches.

Weatherall knocked on the colonel's door, and when a voice said, "Come in," he pushed into the coach proper, where a heavyset man with graying hair waved a greeting. "How'd things go in Pueblo?"

"No trouble getting the supplies."

"See General Sheffield?"

"He sent you his best."

"Well, let's have a drink on that." Colonel Wade Thompson shoved himself to his feet and ambled over to a cabinet. He pulled out a bottle of bourbon and two glasses, then motioned Weatherall to a table in the room's center. As Weatherall sat down, the colonel poured two drinks — four fingers for himself, two for Weatherall. He reached up to his shirt pocket for Long Nines and handed one of the cigars to Weatherall.

Weatherall bit off the end of his cigar and dropped it in a cuspidor. He struck a match and held it to the colonel's cigar. While the colonel puffed, Weatherall studied the man's puffy countenance. Dark circles sagged beneath the colonel's brown eyes, and strain had etched lines from his hairline to his nose.

Weatherall's tongue arched a smoke ring toward the ceiling. The railroad had been having a tough time. He hated to tell the colonel that tougher times lay ahead. "I ran into Bill Baismore in Pueblo."

"So?"

"He said the Colorado's hired a new troubleshooter named Dallas Mason."

"You sound like he means trouble."

"He does. I know Dallas. He's the best."

"Gunman?"

"Among other things."

"What else do you know about him?"

"Dallas is dependable. If he told Adams he'd push that line through, he'll do it."

The colonel dipped the end of his cigar in his bourbon and stared moodily across the car.

"Holy cow. It's just one damn thing after another. I don't want to fight the Colorado, but from what you say, a fight's coming. I've put up with their shenanigans so far — tearing up track, moving survey stakes, mucking up grade. But if they've hired a gunman, we're gonna be forced to take some action. You said you know this person?"

"We used to work together as U.S. marshals out of Denver. A good man to have watching your back."

"Were you two friendly?"

"We were."

"What happened? Why did he leave the law?"

"Same reason I did. He made a mistake."

"And then he put his gun up for hire?"

"I guess he figured that's all he knew. I can understand it. If I hadn't met you, what would I be doing?"

"Not that. You're too good a man to go wrong, Creed."

"Maybe. Maybe not."

He swallowed some bourbon, felt the liquor warm his gut. The colonel's thoughtful gaze dropped to the table; his upper lip drew in as his thoughts drifted elsewhere. Weatherall glanced around the coach, which had been turned into comfortable living quarters. The polished table they sat at was surrounded by four upholstered chairs, while two deep couches covered in brushed green velvet occupied each side of the car. The windows were draped with the same velvet, and a heavy brown deep-pile carpet covered the floor. To the front of the car sat a mahogany liquor cabinet; a potbellied stove occupied one corner. There was a coffeepot on the stove, but the colonel did no cooking here. He ate at a special table in the mess tent with Creed, Charlotte, and the foreman.

Weatherall bit into his cigar. He formed a high, broad-shouldered shape sitting there, and his thoughts were on the colonel. The colonel was worried because the line was three weeks behind, and money was a problem. The news about Dallas didn't set too well either. Up to now there'd been trouble, but no one had been killed. That could change. The Colorado was bringing in someone with Dallas's reputation for one reason: They meant to put the Denver Railroad out of business.

Ever since leaving Denver, each line had engaged in dirty tricks to get the edge, but they hadn't paid off. Now the Colorado meant to become violent.

Tobacco flakes soured Weatherall's mouth, and he spat out a sliver of Long Nine. He was concerned himself. Dallas was a hard man with a well-earned reputation. But Weatherall

12

knew there was one thing he didn't have to worry about: Dallas was no back-shooter. Whatever came would come from the front. Dallas had his own set of rules, and he played by them.

Weatherall swallowed the last of his bourbon. It was too bad Dallas had gone wrong. When they'd been marshals, they'd worked together a number of times and had become close friends. Then, after they'd been fired, they'd gone their separate ways, but over the years news of Dallas had filtered throughout the West. He had the reputation of being a top man with a gun, and that gun was for hire.

A chair squealed as the colonel wheeled around to the table. Cigar smoke wreathed the air, and the rich, heavy smell of bourbon crept outward as the colonel poured two more drinks. Weatherall tongued a smoke ring, watched it float lazily upward. He watched the colonel soak his cigar butt in the bourbon, settle the damp butt between his teeth. He had another bit of bad news to spring on the colonel but hated to do it. The colonel was worried enough.

Weatherall placed both hands on the table. "I heard a rumor in Pueblo that you're not going to like."

"Like what?"

"The Colorado has blocked off Raton Pass. They're supposed to have a bunch of men down there to hold it until their line arrives."

"You think it's true?"

"That's the kind of move Dallas would make."

"Holy cow! If they block that pass, we're finished. There's no other way through those mountains."

"There must be some other way."

"The general surveyed the route and that pass is it."

"Then why didn't he have us set up a crew down there?"

Twin lines wrinkled the colonel's brow. "The Denver line has been trying to play fair, Creed. You know that. The general wanted to avoid gunplay." The colonel shook his head. Doubt furrowed his cheeks. "If we lose this line, General Sheffield's ruined. He's sunk his personal fortune into this railroad, plus a lot of money from his best friends. As you know, we aren't getting a dime from the government. This money was all subscribed. A lot of people are going to end up broke."

Weatherall crossed his legs, shifted around in his chair. "I've never understood why the government wouldn't put up part of the funds. They came through with land and money for the Central Pacific and the Union Pacific."

"The government needed that railroad to open the West. They don't see any profit in a north–south track right now. Colorado is underdeveloped. There's only ten thousand people in the whole state south of Denver. Only five hundred between Denver and Pueblo."

"In other words, the government isn't looking ahead."

"Exactly. That's why the general jumped in. He figured we could build this road and pick up the farms and ranches that will eventually be here, plus sign a contract with the Mexicans to haul their minerals and farm goods into the States. Later he planned to swing a spur west over the Rockies to haul gold and silver from Leadville and the other mining camps. What he didn't figure on was the Colorado making the same plans. We were doing fine until they started paralleling us. I love railroading, Creed. It's my life. Why can't two outfits just make track and let the best man win? Why do we have to have all this infighting?"

"That's the way it goes, Colonel. Something called greed."

The colonel released a long breath as his left hand stroked his beard. His cigar went out and phosphorous flared as he struck a match. Gloom marked his heavy countenance, and when he relit the cigar, his thoughts were obviously elsewhere. After he shook out the match, he glanced over at Weatherall. "This is your end of the business. What are we going to do about Raton Pass?"

"I'll ride down and check things out. Maybe it's not as bad as we think."

"You know the pass?"

"Never been there."

"Rough, rugged terrain, and that pass is a natural walkway through solid rock. Three or four good men could hold that place against an army."

"All I heard was a rumor, Colonel. Maybe we can get there first."

"We'll get there first or not at all. Damn the Colorado. Why can't we just build railroads? But, no, there's always got to be trouble. Sometimes I think I ought to be in another line of work."

"You wouldn't be happy."

"I'm not too happy right now."

Weatherall suppressed a grin at the colonel's pessimism. Things had always worked out for the man as long as Weatherall had known him, although things hadn't always worked out easy.

The colonel hefted the whiskey bottle. "More bourbon?"

"No thanks. I can't handle it like you do.

16

I've got to stay sober enough to meet Charlotte."

"Wonderful woman. You had a stroke of luck when you met her."

"No argument there. How come you never remarried, Colonel?"

"I'm married to the railroad. For me to take another wife wouldn't be fair to the woman. I'll have to admit, though, a few years ago in Sacramento I came close." The colonel dunked his cigar in his bourbon, stuck the cigar in his mouth. "We been together four years. Right?"

"Four years next month."

"They've been good years, Creed. We've accomplished a lot."

"I guess we have."

"I remember the first day you walked into my office. You were uncertain then. Lost. Looking for a new chance at life. I told you you'd take to railroading. Told you to stick with me and you'd have a new career."

"Seems like it worked out that way."

"I knew it would. This is a great life. I don't know anything to beat it. After all these years, I hear an engine hoot and I still feel a thrill shoot down my spine."

"I know what you mean."

The colonel removed his cigar from his teeth and regarded its long ash. "Creed, that thing that happened back in Benbow doesn't still haunt you, does it?"

"No, I've had five years to learn how to live with it."

"Good. You can't carry your mistakes with you, or they'll break you."

Silence fell between the two men. The colonel sucked at his cigar, and Weatherall stared down at the table. Late-afternoon sunlight poured through the window, bringing a freshness to the car. An abrupt breeze whipped up, rattling the panes. Weatherall chewed on his cigar as he thought over the colonel's question. No, he didn't feel guilty anymore about killing Earl Sparks, but he still regretted it. That shooting had been a bad decision, one that had changed the direction of his life. He'd been a lawman since his eighteenth birthday, and that was all he'd ever wanted to be. But Sparks's death had cost Weatherall his badge. That loss had cut the meaning from his life. Then he'd met the colonel, who'd given him a second chance. Better yet, he'd met Charlotte. Since then, he'd had a feeling that things had a way of working out for the best.

Weatherall got to his feet. "I guess I'll be going."

"All right, Creed. See you at supper."

Outside, the sun lay near the horizon to the west. Looking in that direction, Weatherall could see the distant outline of the Rocky Mountains form a hazy barrier against the sky. On a map, those mountains seemed to divide the state, the eastern half being plains country; the west, mountains. The wind brought the aroma of piñon pine and the scent of juniper. Close to the south of the camp, the Arkansas River carved its eastward-moving path.

Weatherall checked his watch. It was ten to five and the mail train and work crew would be in at five-thirty. He wanted to see Charlotte and was glad there was only a short time left. He'd spend that time looking over the town. This was a tough town but as long as whatever was going on didn't interfere with the railroad's progress, it was every man for himself. The men who ran it and the men who played in it knew that. Hardly an individual roamed these streets after dark without arming himself with a gun or knife or both.

As Weatherall strolled the dusty street, he saw Cal Reed and his wife, Norma, standing in front of their R and R Hotel. The hotel served the town's inhabitants, providing room and board at two dollars a day. That price was steep, but in these "hell on wheels" establishments money flowed like wine as railroaders traded their pay for pleasure. Weatherall passed the barbershop, Trueheart's Saloon, and White's Café.

At the end of the street, Weatherall faced Bullard's Emporium. The huge tent was the town's showplace. It had a fifty-foot bar with a mirror reflecting the rows of bottles shelved, flank to flank, along its length. Bullard's had the only dance floor in town, and Amos Bullard had imported thirty girls from Denver to dance with and otherwise entertain his customers. Beyond the saloon, the tents that housed Bullard's women sprawled aimlessly. These tents served as the girls' homes. A lot of money had changed hands in them.

Amos Bullard's bulky form filled the tent door. "Creed. Good to see you back."

"Good to be back."

"How about a drink?"

"I'd better pass. I've had two already."

"Come on in. I've made a change while you were gone."

Weatherall shrugged and stepped inside the huge tent. "I see you got a roulette wheel."

Bullard's pudgy face beamed. His fingers toyed with the heavy watch chain dangling across his vest. "The only one south of Denver. And I've enlarged the dance floor. I can get twenty couples out there now."

"What are you going to do with all your money, Amos?"

"What money? I pay the help, keep the place up. I'm not making any money."

"Amos, you lead a tough life."

Both men laughed and Bullard slapped Weatherall on the shoulder. "Sure you won't have that drink?"

Weatherall shook his head. Bullard was a money grubber, but he ran an honest place. The railroad hands could count on a square deal here. Bullard was hardworking, ambitious, and resourceful, a man who liked his comforts. He could be too flattering at times, and had a short man's need to feel important, but everyone had shortcomings.

"Creed, how are you?"

He swung to his right and saw Nelly May Scott standing at the bar. Nelly May was Bullard's star attraction. She was a beauty whose voice could turn men into dumb cattle. He walked over to the bar to join her. "Little early for you to be working, isn't it?"

Her smile revealed perfect teeth. Her mouth was a red cupid's bow. "What else have I got to do?"

He shrugged, then placed his back to the bar and hooked a boot heel over the railing. Of all the people in camp, Nelly May was the only one he couldn't peg. With her looks, she could have had any man she wanted. It didn't make sense, her being in a place like Bullard's. Yet, from what he'd heard, she'd been a saloon girl for years.

But Nelly May didn't look like a saloon girl. Her features lacked the slyness, the dissipation, the cynical despair that marked the painted countenance of other girls. Nelly May looked fresh and innocent, as if this life had failed to leave its mark on her. But Weatherall knew Nelly May hadn't escaped the brutal scars of prostitution; she had somehow learned to cover them. Still, he never knew quite what to make of her.

She gave a flirty little toss of her blond hair. "I haven't seen you lately."

"Been over to Pueblo."

"How's the big city?"

"Not much to brag about."

"You just get in?"

He nodded.

"I saw your wife go out on the work train about noon."

"I know. I'm just killing time till it gets back."

Nelly May poured herself a drink from the bottle beside her glass. "How long you two been married?"

"Three years."

She lifted her glass. "Here's to you. Maybe it'll last."

"It'll last."

She smiled again, but only with her lips. Her eyes were neutral. "That's what you men always say. . . . Creed, I need a favor."

"If I can."

"I want you to talk to Jim."

"Is it about Tully?"

"Yes."

"Jim's a grown man. I can't tell him what to do."

"Creed, Jim admires you. He looks up to you. Tell him what I am. Tell him it's not worth it."

Weatherall shook his head, stared off across the tent for a long moment. Then his gaze came back to Nelly May. "I can't."

"Why not?"

"I just can't. It's something only a man could understand."

A shadow flitted across Nelly May's finely chiseled features. She sighed regretfully. "You men are such fools. Pride. That's all you know."

"I'm sorry." A train hooted in the distance, and Weatherall pushed off the bar. "I've got to go. Charlotte will be here in a few minutes. Don't worry — things have a way of working out." He left Nelly May staring down into her shot glass.

CHAPTER 2

When the work train screeched to a halt,
young Jim Smith leaped from it and put out
a hand to help Charlotte Weatherall to the
ground. She thanked him, and upon turning
to the front saw Creed striding up track to
greet her. As always, the sight of his wide-
shouldered frame made her heart do flip-
flops. She'd never imagined a woman could
love a man so much. Creed was everything
to her; her life was gray when he was away
but became a golden rush whenever he appeared.

She hurried to meet him, and they stood
there facing each other silently for a moment.
She studied the strong set of his lips; his direct
gray eyes; his hair, black as a locomotive engine. He had proved to be a loyal, affectionate
husband whose love, like hers, grew daily. She
found herself wanting to reach out and touch
him but knew it would look unseemly before
the crowd of track layers breaking around
them. Suddenly she was embarrassed. They'd
been married for three years; it seemed silly

to feel like some foolish schoolgirl every time he came into view.

"Creed, I missed you."

"I missed you, too."

"It's good to have you home."

"I have to leave tomorrow."

She fought back her disappointment. She'd known he was the railroad's troubleshooter when she'd married him. She'd also known what that meant. Besides, he had enough troubles without her complaining. "How long will you be gone?"

"Ten days at least."

"Where are you going?"

"Raton Pass."

"That's over two hundred miles from here."

"I know."

"The railroad's nowhere near the pass. Why go there?"

"I heard a rumor that Adams has a crew down there. The colonel wants it checked out."

"Does it mean gunplay?"

"It does if Adams holds that pass."

"Then, if Adams *is* there, it means fighting?"

"I don't know what to tell you, Charlotte."

"Tell me to forget it. We've got tonight. Let's not waste any of it."

They swung west and strolled the work

train's length, planning to skirt the engine and follow the spur line to their coach. Jim Smith lifted a hand as they passed him, and Tom Love tipped his cap and said, "Good evening, Missus Weatherall." From somewhere in the camp, a dog howled. In one of the saloons, someone banged out "Alabama Gal" on a piano. The heady scents of pine and juniper spiced the breeze, and miles in the distance sunset's deep colors tinted the land.

When Creed and his wife entered the coach the colonel had refurbished for their living quarters, Creed took her arm and drew her against him; they kissed.

He held her at arm's length, and passion burned in his gray eyes. "We could skip the supper."

Her head was buried against his chest. His distinctive man-odor filled her nostrils. Finally, she tipped her head back. "We'd get mighty hungry around midnight."

"You're right, as usual. Why don't we stop at Ernie's and get a bottle of wine after supper."

"You know just what to say, don't you?"

"I try."

"Creed, I'm so dirty. I'll need a bath after supper."

He nodded. "I could use one myself. I'll have the cook heat some water while we eat.

Now go wash up."

She went to the bedroom and filled the porcelain bowl with water. The pitcher and bowl were a wedding gift from the colonel. She washed her hands and face with Pearl soap, dried them, then opened the window and dashed the soapy water on the ground. It was dark now, and a spotty line of piñons silhouetted the western sky. The river's low murmur reached her while the coolness of early evening crept through the open window.

After a moment, she stepped back to the washstand and poured a fresh bowl of water for Creed. He would need to wash up too.

The odors of black coffee, fried beef, and fried potatoes mingled in the mess tent as Charlotte and Creed entered. They angled toward the colonel's table. Sitting with him were Jess Strawberry, the track foreman, and Will Johnson, the rolling-stock boss. All three men got to their feet in a show of courtesy and stood there until Charlotte was seated. The colonel nodded while Strawberry and Johnson murmured, "Good evening, Missus Weatherall." As the men sat down, the colonel waved a hand at a mess attendant, who swung into the kitchen for their food.

While they waited, the colonel drummed his fingers impatiently and the two foremen kept their gazes on their plates. Charlotte glanced around the huge tent. It sheltered about a hundred men, who sat at rough wooden tables. Tin plates were nailed to those tables; after meals, one of the cook's helpers walked around the room carrying a mop and a pail of soapy water and swabbed out the dirty plates.

The men seated around these tables were of every size and description. Many of them were hard, tough, dangerous characters, little removed from desperadoes. Being so far from the civilizing effects of law, order, and public opinion, they resorted nightly to drinking, gambling, whoring, and fighting. Of course, some of them were men of good character. Decent, loyal individuals, proud of their railroad careers and dimly aware of the part they played in the unifying of a nation. Charlotte knew most of the men by name. They treated her with unfailing respect and accepted her as one of their own.

The mess attendant arrived and forked out fried beef, potatoes, and bread. It was plain but hearty fare that never varied, and was washed down with strong, black coffee. As the attendant served them, Creed said, "Tell the cook I need a couple of tubs of hot water."

They ate in silence, but Charlotte, who was not hungry, picked at her food. At the table beyond, she spotted Jim Smith, who had worked the Central Pacific track with the colonel. Next to him sat Tom Love, a chubby, cheerful man who had come west with the Union Pacific. Of all the crew, these two were her favorites — Jim, for his sincerity; Tom, for his outgoing personality. Her gaze found Al Swanson, the mess attendant. Al was a former track hand turned alcoholic. Al was seldom sober and even more seldom dependable, but he had helped shove the Central Pacific over the High Sierras, so the colonel kept him on.

After supper, the colonel handed out smokes. He held a match to his cigar tip, puffed the cigar to a red glow, then leaned back in his chair as Al brought fresh coffee. "Jess, how much track did we make today?"

"Three miles. Same as yesterday."

"Three's enough for right now. Fact is, in a couple of weeks we may not be making any."

Jess leaned forward. "I don't get you."

"Creed heard a rumor that Adams has sealed off the pass."

Strawberry straightened in his chair and muttered something under his breath. Johnson's gaze shifted around the table as his expression sobered. Weatherall sat passively, and strain formed a small pocket around the table. The only sound was voices rumbling up from the track crew's tables. Charlotte took a slim cigar from her shirt pocket, and Strawberry held his Long Nine's glowing tip to hers for a light. She knew Creed disapproved of her smoking; he had asked her to quit. However, she saw no need to give up something she enjoyed. Besides, he smoked. She'd promised to quit when he did, and had heard no more about it.

Johnson removed the cigar from his mouth and cleared his throat. "If that rumor's true, we're out of business."

The colonel nodded. "That's right."

Strawberry glanced across at Weatherall. "You're not sure of this?"

"No. But it makes sense. We're making more track than Adams, but if he holds the pass, our progress won't make any difference."

Strawberry's teeth clamped into his cigar. "General Sheffield could lose his shirt. I can't see him doing that without a fight."

"Neither can I," added Johnson.

Charlotte glanced at her husband's pensive countenance. "What do you think, Creed?"

"The general's a fighter."

"Holy cow!" the colonel yelped. "I almost stuck my cigar in my coffee."

The others laughed, knowing the colonel's penchant for soaking his cigar in bourbon.

Down the way, chairs scraped as men pushed back from tables. Footsteps echoed as those men hiked for the doorway. Tom Love yelled for more coffee, and someone banged metal objects together in the kitchen area.

The colonel's long, powerful fingers stroked his beard. "If Adams controls that pass, an army couldn't take it."

Strawberry unconsciously scratched his belly. His brown eyes narrowed. "What about all that money the general and his friends put up? They can't afford to back off."

The colonel shook his head. "Our grading crew's only thirty miles from the pass, and it looks like we'll beat the Colorado there by days. But if Creed's right, it doesn't matter. We're railroad men, not gunfighters."

Johnson cleared his throat again. "What are you going to do?"

"Hope for the best while Creed checks things out."

"I hate to think of making track when it may be a lot of work for nothing," Strawberry muttered.

The colonel shrugged. "Making track is what you get paid for. And let's keep this among ourselves."

Strawberry nodded while Johnson fiddled with a shirt button. Weatherall sat upright in his chair, big shoulders square as cigar smoke drifted from his nostrils. Charlotte considered her cigar for a moment, then glanced across the mess tent. Most of the men had departed, but a half-dozen track hands still occupied the tables. The tent served coffee until ten o'clock and doubled as a recreation center for those men who preferred to play checkers, write letters, or talk rather than roam the town or return to the crowded sleeping cars. Lamplight flashed off Jim Smith's yellow hair, and his boyish features were animated as he made a point to Tom Love.

At a table below Smith and Love, Tully Williams got to his feet. He lined his testy, quarrelsome face in their direction. "Smith, keep out of Bullard's tonight."

Jim glanced in Tully's direction. He wet his lips but didn't answer.

"See that you keep away from my girl; I'm tired of telling you."

Tom Love held up both hands placatingly. "Come off it, Tully. Nelly May's nobody's girl unless they've got the price of a drink or a dance ticket. Why don't you leave Jim alone?"

Tully's top teeth gleamed. "Why don't you mind your own business?" After a final glare in Jim's direction, Tully wheeled around and stalked from the tent.

Weatherall flipped the ashes from his cigar.

He glanced at the colonel. "You've got a mean one there. Why don't you fire him?"

"He does his job."

"He's a troublemaker."

"Creed, I like Jim too, but a man has to stand on his own two feet. You know that."

"I guess you're right. But Jim's worth ten like Tully."

The colonel waved for some hot coffee. "Shall we give Jess and Will the rest of the bad news?"

Strawberry glanced from the colonel to Weatherall and back to the colonel. "You mean there's more?"

"Afraid so. Adams has got himself a new troubleshooter. Fellow named Dallas Mason."

Johnson let out a low whistle. "Mason. I know him from up north. He's nothing but a common murderer."

"I wouldn't say that," Weatherall murmured.

"I would. I saw him shoot a man in cold blood in Salt Lake City."

"You trying to tell me Dallas didn't give that man a chance?"

"Mason called his man out, if that's what you mean. It was about sunrise. As a matter of fact, Mason's called so many men out at daybreak that some people call him Sunrise. It was still cold-blooded murder. The other

33

fellow didn't have a chance."

Weatherall frowned down at his plate. The cigar had gone dead in his mouth without his knowing it. Charlotte felt a sharp pain close around her heart. She didn't want to hear any more of this, and she felt Creed didn't either. "Gentlemen, I'm a little tired. I think Creed and I will call it a night."

The three railroad men came to their feet as Weatherall and Charlotte pushed back from the table. They said good night, then walked across the tent. When they reached Jim Smith and Tom Love, Weatherall paused, leaned between the two men, and said something Charlotte didn't catch.

Then the couple left the tent and stood under starry skies. Weatherall said, "Wait here. I'll get the wine," and walked away.

The street boiled with men. From her experience with the railroad, Charlotte knew that every sort of individual imaginable toured the street: pimp, prostitute, thief, and murderer followed the tracks. This town was worse than most because it served two competing lines. About three hundred yards to the east, she could see the lights of the rival Colorado camp; tracklayers from both camps ducked in and out of the tents and false-fronted shacks spread out in disorderly fashion. This place had been aptly named. It was truly "hell on wheels," for only greed and avarice operated here.

A hand touched her shoulder. Weatherall said, "Let's go home," and they retraced their steps around the work engine. Once inside their coach, Weatherall set the wine on the table, removed his Stetson, and gave her his smile. "The night's still young."

Before she could answer, someone knocked. Creed opened the door and waved in Jim Smith, Tom Love, and two men she recognized but could not name. They carried two tubs of water. Weatherall pointed at the curtains partitioning off the coach. "Put one tub in there, the other one in here."

The tubs were duly placed and as the men departed, Weatherall said, "Thanks." Smith and the others nodded; Tom Love said, "Any time I can be of service, just call on me." He glanced at Charlotte, said, "Good night, Missus Weatherall," and closed the door behind him.

"That Tom Love is the sweetest man," Charlotte said.

"I might not use those words, but Tom's a good man."

"Creed, do you think that Scott woman will cause trouble between Jim and Tully?"

"It looks like it."

"I can't understand her. Why would she

want to cause trouble?"

"She doesn't. Tully does."

"I feel sorry for Jim. He's just a boy."

"He might be more man than you think. Anyway, it's his trouble. He has to handle it. Let's get our baths before the water gets cold."

Charlotte walked into the curtained-off end of the coach, undressed, and sank into the washtub. She wished she had a real tub, but a person had to rough it when railroading. She wet the washrag, squeezed warm water over her shoulders. Her hands worked with the washrag and soap, but her thoughts drifted back three and a half years. She hadn't liked Creed when they'd first met. He'd seemed too sure, too confident. Then she'd realized a man in his position had to be confident. Otherwise, he couldn't have faced the danger that constantly dogged him. She'd seen the kind side of him the night he'd warned Buck Weaton to quit annoying a worn-down saloon girl named Kate. Afterward, he'd brought Kate coffee and an extra blanket for the cold ride over the Sierras. His thoughtfulness had impressed her, because most men didn't bother with a woman like Kate except for one reason. Another thing that had impressed her was the courage he'd shown in bracing up to Buck, who was a born killer.

Her thoughts turned to the present. Anticipation of tonight made her flush. Her physical reaction to Creed never ceased to amaze her. She'd been married before, but she hadn't experienced anything like this. And Jack had been a good husband. They'd lived a good life.

One night when she was working as a singer she had met Jack, a professional gambler. Soon afterward, they'd married. He'd taught her all he knew, which was plenty, and they'd worked the saloons and gambling halls of San Francisco until Jack had dropped dead dealing a hand of stud. The doctor had not known what killed him. Jack was only twenty-five and seemingly in perfect health. His death had shaken her. She'd lost her certainty about life. She'd been afraid, vulnerable. She'd wanted to get out of Frisco, and her chance had come when she was offered a job dealing in Ken Bennett's tent with a hell-on-wheels town that followed the Central Pacific.

She hadn't expected to ever feel alive again, so it was wonderful to discover that love could happen twice. Still, it was strange that she could have loved two such different men. Jack had been thin, dark-skinned, handsome, with laughing eyes and a ready grin. Both men were affectionate, but Jack had been spoiled and immature, whereas Creed was neither. Jack's way of life meant being on the go, and he had the professional gambler's cynical outlook on human frailties. Creed loved to stay home and tended to overlook his fellow man's shortcomings. Finally, where Jack had always been cool and deliberate, Creed was a somewhat impetuous individual whose temper often overruled his better judgment.

The tips of Charlotte's fingers trailed through the water. Creed was a steady hand with a gun and could hit what he aimed at, but he was no gunslinger. If this Dallas was as fast as Will had intimated, Creed was far from his match. She'd suffered through this kind of situation once before, but in those days she hadn't been Creed's wife. His death then would have hurt, but now it would rip her apart. She would never forget the day Creed had faced Buck Weaton. No one thought Creed had a chance. He hadn't outdrawn Buck, he'd outsmarted him. Buck had been a thumb-buster. He had filed the trigger from his revolver so that he could draw, depress the hammer, and release it in one swift motion. Such a draw was made in a flash, but it lacked accuracy outside a radius of about five feet. Creed had known this, so when he reached a point about twenty feet from Buck, he drew his revolver. Buck had fired several rounds before Creed fired once, but his shot had hit Buck's heart.

Creed's voice cut through the curtain. "Charlotte, if you don't hurry up, it'll be time for me to leave for Raton Pass."

She pushed aside her worries and started to scrub vigorously. "All right, Creed. I'll be done in a minute."

CHAPTER 3

Weatherall reined in the mare at the entrance to the Pass of the Rat. It had been uphill traveling, and a brief rest wouldn't hurt either of them. To the west, he could see the bulky outline of the Sangre de Cristo mountains, and Trinchera Peak's thirteen and a half thousand feet shimmered on the skyline. South of Trinchera lay Culebra Peak's five-hundred-foot-higher outline. This was mountainous country; compared to the western skyline, Raton Pass was a measly cut through the eight-thousand-foot mass of the Raton Range separating Colorado from New Mexico.

Weatherall glanced back toward Trinidad. He'd spent the night there, happy to get a hot bath, a hot shave, and a comfortable bed. It had been the first decent night's sleep he'd enjoyed for five days. He remembered a time when he used to enjoy nights on the trail. Nights of hot coffee spiked with whiskey, the relaxing taste of a good cigar. But he'd been younger then. Now the coffee was too bitter, the cigar too strong, and the ground too hard.

Worst of all, he missed Charlotte. Whatever appeal the trail might have had for him was gone. All he wanted was to get this trip over with and go home. He never wanted to sleep alone again as long as he lived.

He'd learned a few things in Trinidad, however. The people there favored the Colorado line over the Denver. The Denver people were going to have to remember there was more to building a railroad than laying track and cutting grade. The general was going to have to send a public relations crew to Trinidad to talk up what the Denver road could do that the Colorado couldn't. This knowledge alone made the trip worthwhile, but he'd heard something else, something that supported the rumor going around Pueblo. Two weeks ago three hard cases from the Colorado had stopped in Trinidad, liquored up, and bragged that they were taking over Raton Pass. They'd left town in the company of a Trinidad saloon woman.

They were obviously at Dad Levison's Inn. Dad, who had been in this country since fur-trapping days, had gained a charter for a toll road that taxed everyone traveling through the pass, and he had build an inn to accommodate them. If the Colorado bunch held the pass, it meant that Dad had thrown in with them.

41

Weatherall clucked the mare forward, and they entered the saddle-backed trail that led through the mountains. His thoughts flickered over the people who had used this natural break: frontiersmen, trappers, traders, Comanche war parties, wagon trains, and now railroaders.

Midday sun beat down on his shoulders, but coolness would arrive with nightfall. Somewhere among these crags a chickadee sang its slender melody. The mare's shoes clacked against rocky underfooting. The pass was slippery and uneven, and it was too narrow to accommodate two railroads. If the men ahead represented the Colorado, the Denver line was a dead dream.

A reedy voice drifted in from Weatherall's left. "Hold up."

Weatherall drew rein. He shifted in the saddle so that he could see the thin figure that moved in on him from the rocky bluffs. A kid, maybe twenty, whose twin revolvers lined in about chest height.

"What's your business?" the kid asked.

Weatherall pushed his Stetson back, studying the kid curiously. He saw a boy trying to act like a man, but not too convincingly. He saw uncertainty in the kid's shifty brown eyes, anxiety in his pale, unlined face. The kid's long hair, a dirty blond, shimmered in the breeze and his lower lip kept pulling in between his teeth.

A click sounded as the kid cocked his right-hand revolver. "I asked you a question."

"Just riding through."

"Riding where?"

"South. Plan to stop at Raton tonight."

The kid's narrow brow contracted. His lower lip drew in again.

Weatherall sat quite still in his saddle. The kid didn't seem to know exactly what he was supposed to do. But his fear made him far more dangerous than he would normally be. Weatherall didn't want to make any move that might spook the youngster.

"I think we'd better go up to the inn. Get off the mare. We'll walk in."

After Weatherall dismounted, he took the reins and meandered south. He could hear the kid following him, but he didn't look back. There were three men here, supposedly. He could only hope the other two were as green as this kid. If so, they couldn't hold this pass. They lacked the know-how. He kept wondering why the fellow at Trinidad had called them hard cases. But one thing was certain: The Colorado had settled in.

The pass twisted right, and as they rounded a bend, Weatherall saw a rocky enclave to his left. In the enclave's center sat a two-story

43

building constructed from rough notched pine logs with mud-chinked filling. The building had a peaked roof to avoid heavy accumulations of snow. To Weatherall's surprise, the windows were glass, giving a strangely incongruous appearance to such an otherwise primitive place. Out to the north, he spotted a weatherbeaten barn with a corral holding six horses.

The kid said, "Tie your horse to the hitching rail."

After Weatherall complied, he swung around to face his captor. The kid looked thinner than ever. The revolvers seemed too big for his hands. The breeze ruffled his shoulder-length hair, and his shifty gaze gleamed with satisfaction.

"Inside." He gestured with one gun barrel.

Weatherall about-faced and trooped ahead until he pushed through the door into the building. At his entrance, a man turned around at the bar, and Weatherall felt a tightening across his chest. He knew this fellow: O.K. Powell. He'd had trouble with him in the past, and the grin breaking across the man's pitted cheeks wasn't one of welcome. Glancing right, Weatherall locked gazes with a tall black-haired individual who sat at a table holding a deck of cards. This one had icewater eyes, a broken nose, large ears, and a square visage. What impressed Weatherall was the man's gunbelt. It was black, with a silver buckle, and cartridge loops made from white leather. Only a man completely sure of his ability would dare strap on such a contraption.

"O.K., I got one," the kid said.

The fellow at the bar nodded. "You sure as hell did. Do you know who this is? It's Creed Weatherall. The big noise of the Denver line. How about a drink, Creed?"

Weatherall shrugged. "A little early, but why not."

His boots hammered out short echoes as he strolled to the bar, and he could feel the black-haired man at the table watching him all the way. As Weatherall approached the bar, Dad Levison emerged from a curtained-off area behind the bar.

"Down here it's Taos Lightning or nothing," O.K. said.

Weatherall settled his weight on the bar and met O.K.'s gaze, a gaze as hard as emeralds. Five years hadn't changed O.K. much. He had the same sly eyes, acne-pitted cheeks, pug nose, muscular body. Though a little gray now threaded his black hair, he no doubt had the same mean, sadistic streak that in the past had propelled him from one violent act to another.

Old man Levison set a bottle of white whiskey and two glasses on the bar. Then he took four steps backward, his faded eyes alert with concern. Weatherall poured a drink and pushed the bottle in Powell's direction. While O.K. poured his drink, Weatherall surveyed the surroundings. At twelve o'clock a flight of stairs led to the upper landing, which was empty. Beyond the stairs was a curtained-off area, and at three o'clock there was a huge fireplace. Indian blankets and mounted elk and deer heads decorated the rough walls on each side of the fireplace. A man played solitaire at the first of the six tables arranged in rows of threes fronting the fireplace. Weatherall looked toward the front door, where the kid stood uneasily.

"Not much like El Paso," O.K. said to Weatherall.

"A lot cooler, as a matter of fact."

"You made me and Buck Weaton look pretty small there. You shouldn't have run us out of town that way."

"I didn't have much choice."

O.K. twirled his glass on the bar. He picked it up, stared down at the wet circle for a long moment. When his head rose, his thick lips parted, revealing heavy, tobacco-browned teeth. "Things are a bit different. You ain't wearing that piece of tin."

"That's exactly what Buck Weaton said."

"I heard you killed Buck. The question is, How? You couldn't take Buck head-on."

"Maybe I got lucky."

"I got a feeling your luck has run out. Right, Rod?"

A noncommittal grunt came from the card-player, but he laid his cards down and gave his full attention to the bar area.

Weatherall dipped his head slightly and surveyed the room from beneath lowered lids. His heart held its steady thump, but the inside of his mouth felt dry. Out of the corner of one eye, he saw Dad Levison step farther back from the bar, and the old-timer's fingers interlaced across his huge stomach. Rod still sat at the table, but his back had straightened and his shoulders had squared. The kid hunched uncertainly just inside the doorway, his lower lip sliding continuously over his upper one. O.K. Powell still stood against the bar, whiskey glass in his right hand.

Somehow Weatherall worked up a little saliva in his mouth. His chances didn't look good; moreover, they weren't apt to improve. Weatherall knew he would have to take Rod out first. He also knew that the calm-faced gunhand understood exactly what he was thinking. Yet Rod hadn't even bothered to stand up. Such confidence was unnerving.

Weatherall knew that if he was lucky enough to down Rod, his chances of turning his revolver back to the front before O.K. could reach his pistol were negligible. As for the kid, he presented the smallest problem. His swaggering gait and tied-down holsters were only an attempt at toughness. If the kid saw Rod and O.K. go down, he would bolt for the horses.

O.K.'s grin widened. "Before you try anything foolish, you'd better take another look at the landing."

Weatherall's gaze lifted, and shock rippled across the small of his back. Standing next to the staircase was a bearded man who lifted his left hand, from which a quirt dangled, in mock salute.

"That's Walt Clanton. Put your gunbelt on the bar, Creed."

Unbuckling his gunbelt, Weatherall lay it on the bar, whereupon O.K. grabbed it and pulled it beyond Weatherall's reach. Boot leather scraped against wood, and Dad Levison eased forward. He reached under the bar to pull out a wool overcoat, which he threw over his left arm. Then he stepped back to the wall, lifted the rifle from its pegs, and shuffled around Weatherall's end of the bar. "I'm going to spend a couple of days in Raton, O.K. You take care of things."

As the old frontiersman scuffed through the doorway and swung right, Weatherall leaned back against the bar. Perspiration wet the sweatband of his Stetson. Levison was no fool — he understood what was about to happen. Weatherall fumbled for a cigar, brought it to his lips. He bit off the end, spat it on the floor. The sour odor of phosphorus sharpened the air as he held a match to the cigar. He kept his hand steady, and he'd been in enough tight spots to know that his face revealed nothing.

Weatherall quickly sized up the distances between him and O.K. Powell and Rod, and how long it would take to reach the doorway. The bearded fellow upstairs balanced himself on forearms resting on the railing. His quirt dangled free from his left wrist, and his mocking gaze never left Weatherall's face. Rod, who had returned to his solitaire, held an uplifted card in his right hand. Weatherall guessed Rod could drop that card, draw, and fire before most men could clear leather. The kid had inched up to stand by Rod's table. Weatherall thought he saw sweat bead the kid's upper lip, then realized the blond-headed punk was trying to grow a mustache.

Cigar smoke stung the insides of Weatherall's mouth. His teeth ached from pressure. Desperation rose in his throat. For a moment he entertained the insane notion of flinging himself at the window five feet away, but he quelled that idea. He'd be dead before he covered half the distance.

"What about that drink?" O.K. said.

Weatherall's gaze shifted to the bar. He picked up his glass of Taos Lightning and downed it, grimacing as the alcohol burned his throat, hit his stomach like liquid fire.

O.K. sat his glass on the bar. "The stuff's not fit to drink, but it's all Dad's got." He pulled a plug of Twist and a clasp knife from his pocket, sliced off a chunk of tobacco, and tucked it between his teeth and gum. Folding the knife, he replaced it in his pocket and sucked at the plug of Twist. "I never did like you, Creed, but I gave you more credit than to come down here alone."

Something clicked in Weatherall's brain. He tongued a perfect smoke ring toward the ceiling. "Who said I came alone?"

O.K. scuffed at his nose. He considered Weatherall carefully, then nodded toward the tables. "Kid, you see anyone else?"

The kid's Adam's apple jerked up and down. "I watched him for a half a mile before he hit the pass. He didn't have any company."

O.K. looked back at Weatherall, sucked on his chew. "Nice try, but nobody's buying."

Cigar smoke trickled from Weatherall's

nostrils. He looked O.K. full in the face. "There's ten men waiting for me back in Trinidad. If I'm not back by tomorrow, you'll be seeing some company."

"You're a liar. Ten men couldn't take this pass."

"They could now. The pass is wide open."

The tobacco formed a lump in O.K.'s cheek. He glanced down at the bar. Rod looked up from his card game. His slim features remained bland and unruffled, but his sudden indifference to the cards told Weatherall another story. The kid began to shift his weight from one foot to the other, and he wiped at his trickle of mustache. On the landing, the fellow with the quirt straightened to his full height. His lips pursed and showed redly through his beard. "You'd better get back out on the trail, kid."

"I been out there all morning. Let somebody else take a turn."

Walt slammed the top of the landing with his quirt. "I said move and I mean now."

The kid made a whining noise, but he spun off through the door.

Weatherall blew out a stream of cigar smoke. "I thought you were in charge of this show, O.K."

"I am, but Walt likes to ride the kid."

Rod grunted bemusedly. "Walt's a regular

51

terror with women and kids."

Weatherall's gaze lifted. He saw a flush spread up from Clanton's beard, saw the man's dark eyes burn with resentment. Another click echoed in Weatherall's brain. His remark about Trinidad had expanded his time frame. They wouldn't dare kill him before morning. True, ten men couldn't take this pass, but they could raise questions about his whereabouts. Embarrassing questions. He had to use what tools he had and hope for the best. He'd already cut the odds against him from four to three, although he would have preferred that Clanton or Rod had gone to guard the pass instead of the kid.

O.K.'s fingers tapped the bar. "I understand you're a married man."

"So?"

"Just thinking out loud. You know, it'd be a shame if your wife never found out what happened to you. There's a hundred ravines in these mountains where somebody could dump a body and no one would ever find it."

A hollow feeling spread over Weatherall's stomach. Dryness crinkled the inside of his mouth again. He understood that O.K. wanted to get a rise out of him.

O.K.'s voice lowered confidentially. "You know, Creed, Mr. Adams didn't spell out exactly what I was supposed to do when you showed up. If you try, you might be able to talk your way out of this. See the little woman again."

"What do I have to do?"

"You might try begging."

Weatherall wasn't fooled by O.K.'s buffoonery. The only way he'd leave this room was feet first.

"Well, Creed, still got your backbone, I see. I mean to break you before this is over."

Rod placed a card on the table, his attention back on the game. "You're wasting your time, O.K.," he said.

"I don't think so. He's thinking about his wife right now. Worrying about how she's going to take the news. Creed, you made me crawl out of El Paso. I mean to even the score."

Weatherall puffed casually on the cigar, determined to control the anxiety ripping his guts. He'd made a serious mistake in turning over his gunbelt. At least he could have taken one or two of them with him. Now he was a piece of meat hanging on a fence. O.K. could do whatever he wanted.

"You know, Creed, I just had a thought. Maybe after this is all over, I could drop by and console the widow."

Weatherall's gut burned. Rage tightened his powerful shoulders, rolled his big hands into massive fists. O.K. caught the reaction. When he grinned, something in Weatherall said, To hell with it, and he took one swift step forward and sank his fist deep in the pit of O.K.'s belly. The plug of tobacco flew out of O.K.'s popped-open mouth. His cheeks turned the color of a dirty bar of soap, and he sagged at the middle. Weatherall drove a left hook into O.K.'s temple. As O.K.'s eyeballs rolled up and back, he sank to one knee. When his hand grappled for the bar for support, Weatherall's right arm drew back for a finishing right cross, but a soft "That'll be all" stopped him.

Weatherall's head jerked in Rod's direction. The slim gunman was standing, his hands dangling at his sides. His clean-shaven visage remained impassive, but a warning flashed from his blue eyes. Rage clogged Weatherall's throat. A wildness shook him. He wanted to hit O.K. Hit him and hit him and hit him until O.K.'s acne-pocked face turned to a mass of bleeding flesh and broken bones. But caution prevailed over Weatherall's animal need to destroy.

With an effort, Weatherall forced himself to step back. He watched the shaken O.K. struggle to regain his feet.

Weatherall looked at the upstairs landing, where Walt Clanton leaned forward with both hands on the railing. Clanton's mean little eyes glared over the distance; he waited for O.K. to regain his senses and punish the man who'd inflicted his beating. Rod had dropped back into his chair. His left hand held the deck of cards, and he appeared to concentrate on the four rows of cards arranged on the table.

O.K.'s head rammed Weatherall's chest, driving him backwards. While Weatherall fought to retain his balance, O.K. slugged him in the ear, the mouth, the side of the throat. O.K. flailed away with both fists. When Weatherall moved in to smother his punches, O.K. connected with the point of Weatherall's chin.

Weatherall's knees unhinged. The muscles in his thighs turned soft. He grabbed O.K.'s shoulders to keep from falling and hung on desperately as the room whirled around him. O.K. tried to push Weatherall away. He hit him with rights and lefts. He butted him in the neck. But Weatherall's fingers clung to O.K.'s shirt. He knew that if his hold loosened, he would go down, and if he went down, O.K. would put the boots to him.

Suddenly, O.K. stopped punching and staggered back against the bar. Weatherall released him. Both men used the bar for support. Their open mouths, glazed eyes, and heaving chests gave mute testimony to their exhaustion. Weatherall drew a hand across his lips. Blood smeared his fingers, and he pulled out his handkerchief and wiped his nose. His upper and lower lip had burst, and blood's salty taste bittered his tongue.

O.K. poured another glass of Taos Lightning, downed it in one gulp. He glared at Weatherall. "I should have used a knee on you."

Weatherall leaned over, picked up his hat, and laid it on the bar. "You would have if you could."

O.K. swung around, rested both forearms on the bar. He rubbed the side of his face; a lump there marked where Weatherall had hit him. O.K.'s gaze dropped to the floor, and he stared at nothing for a long minute. Then his head lifted. "Walt, get that woman of yours down here. I'm hungry."

Weatherall's gaze rocketed to the landing. He watched as Clanton stumped over to the nearest room and hammered on the door. "Ruby Lee, get downstairs. We want some vittles."

Seconds later a flaxen-haired young woman in a faded, short-sleeved yellow dress stepped into the hallway. When she passed Clanton, he slashed her across the back with his quirt. "I said *move*, Ruby Lee."

Although the quirt struck so hard that Weatherall winced, the woman's angular features remained as stolid as a Ute squaw's. Her high heels tapped down the stairs with Clanton lumbering behind her. When she reached the first floor, she was close enough that Weatherall could see the swollen side of her face, her blackened eyes, and the dark bruises on her upper arms. She gave Weatherall one quick glance before rounding into the curtained-off area which contained the kitchen.

The pungent odor of burning pine rose from the kitchen. Pots rattled behind the curtain. O.K. played with his whiskey glass as Clanton impatiently slapped his quirt against the side of one leg. Weatherall wiped his nose again, and his handkerchief came away clean. Ruby Lee had looked self-contained, but she must have been terrified. Weatherall wondered why she had accompanied this bunch in the first place. He also wondered about her chances of leaving here alive. She'd be a witness to his killing, but unlike Dad, who'd fled to Raton, she couldn't leave.

The tip of Weatherall's tongue touched the inside of his upper lip. The lip was swollen and it hurt to the touch. He looked at Clanton, completely understanding the man's loutish character. Weatherall had met many Clantons:

braggarts and bullies with yellow streaks as wide as their backs. He acted tough, but was dangerous only when he stood behind you.

Clanton balanced his quirt between both hands. "O.K., what about those men in Trinidad?"

"There are no men in Trinidad."

"Suppose you're wrong?"

"Then we hit them in the pass. We can set up a field of fire a snake couldn't crawl through."

Clanton flexed his quirt. He glanced at Weatherall, then back to O.K. "You let him off too easy. I'd have broken him up a bit."

"He's yours any time you want him."

A snicker from Rod's table whipped Clanton's attention in that direction. The side of his neck colored, and as much of his face as Weatherall could see through the man's whiskers. Clanton resembled a dog straining at a leash. His hands arced the quirt until Weatherall thought it would break. Clanton's hatred for Rod, who so casually studied the cards laid out before him, was so intense that it deformed Clanton's face. Clanton ached to hurt, to destroy. His square frame almost shook with impotent rage, but Rod didn't give him so much as a glance. His anger flamed higher.

Abruptly, Clanton spun back to Weatherall. "What are you looking at?"

"Not much."

Rod snickered again, and Clanton's quirt slashed empty air. "You watch your tongue or I'll strip your hide off."

Laughter sounded from the table as Rod's head tilted attentively. "When he rams that quirt down your throat, don't look for me to pull him off you."

Words caught in Clanton's throat. He swung blindly off to his right and shouldered into the kitchen. Four loud explosions followed: flesh striking flesh.

Weatherall brought his hands together and looked down at his interlocked fingers. He should have kept his mouth shut. His remark had been the thumb that cocked the hammer, and Clanton had been forced to pull the trigger on somebody. The only possible somebody was Ruby Lee. Weatherall felt a little sick. That woman had enough problems without his making more. He glanced over at O.K. "I gave you more credit. How'd you hook up with that trash?"

O.K. shrugged. "He has his uses."

High-heeled shoes tapped against flooring as Ruby Lee edged through the curtain, carrying dishes, cups, silverware. She set the table behind Rod and walked back to the

59

kitchen, to return with a tray holding a large platter, a steaming bowl, and a blackened coffeepot.

Walt Clanton followed her to the table and took the chair with its back to the wall. Weatherall and O.K. trooped over and sat down as Rod took the chair to Clanton's left. This put Weatherall facing Clanton, with O.K. seated to his right.

Ruby Lee shrank into the niche between the fireplace and the wood box. Weatherall sensed that she'd fade into the wall if she could. Suddenly her lids drew down, and she met his gaze fully. He thought he saw something flicker in her eyes, as if she were trying to tell him something, yet her features remained completely impassive.

Clanton forked a piece of beef onto his plate. O.K. spooned up some beans, passed the bowl to Weatherall.

After the men had filled their plates, they ate quickly and quietly. Finishing, Rod pushed his chair back from the table and punched tobacco into a corncob pipe. He lit it and the bitter smell of tobacco rose in white-wreathed smoke. "I'll relieve the kid. He hasn't had anything to eat since morning." Rod stood up and removed a brown Stetson from a hat rack; wind rustled through the doorway as he stepped outside.

O.K. stuck a fresh plug of Twist into his mouth. He glanced at Walt Clanton, who held a match to a cigar. "Escort our guest upstairs. He needs a chance to think things out. Remember what I said, Creed. There still might be a chance to see the little woman if you play the right part."

After Weatherall got to his feet, Clanton stood up. He put his left hand on his gun butt, motioned toward the stairs. Weatherall picked up his Stetson and, clapping it on his head, walked to the staircase. As he climbed, he heard Clanton clump along behind. About halfway up the stairs, Weatherall slowed his pace. He hoped that Clanton wouldn't notice, and would close the distance between them. If that happened, he would wheel back on Clanton, slug him, and grab for his revolver. It wasn't much of a chance, but it might be the only one he got. Rod and the kid were outside. With luck, O.K., who was a dead shot but a slow draw, might be caught by surprise. But Clanton was no fool. He maintained his distance.

At the top of the stairs, Weatherall hesitated. "Room seven," Clanton said. Weatherall crossed the landing and opened the door. It was a typical hotel room, with a bed, table, chair, lamp, and chamber pot — except the room's one window had been sealed with heavy planking. Clanton said, "Light the lamp," and as Weatherall held a match to the wick, the door closed and a key rattled in the lock.

Weatherall replaced the lamp's glass shade. He walked to the window, placed his shoulder against the planking, and shoved with all the force of his two hundred and twenty pounds. It was wasted effort, so he dropped his hat on the table and lay back on the bed with his hands clasped under his head. He might as well relax. He wasn't going anywhere.

CHAPTER 4

When Jim Smith strolled into Bullard's tent, Nelly May Scott's vibrant alto voice hit the first note of "I'll Take You Home Again, Kathleen," one of the railroad men's favorite tunes. Jim paused just inside the doorway, his gaze fast on Nelly May's black-clad figure. She stood at the dance floor's far side, accompanied by Marv Green, Bullard's bald-headed, cigar-chomping piano player. The tables were full. The bar was lined with railroad men and saloon women. Even though the crowd was large, it was quiet, a tribute to Nelly May's magnetism. When she sang, men listened, and saloon girls welcomed the chance to stop play-acting for a few moments.

Jim weaved his way through the crowd to an empty table fronting the dance floor. From here, he had a perfect view of Nelly May's striking face and figure. He dropped into a chair, wondering for the thousandth time what a woman like her was doing in this dirt-floored tent. Leaning back, he forgot the hushed crowd, the glitzy surroundings. He forgot everything but this woman, and the way her voice created a yearning directly in the center of his chest.

A hand dropped on his shoulder, and he looked up to see Amos Bullard's short, chunky form standing next to him. Amos said, "She's something, isn't she?"

"You'll get no argument from me."

Amos fiddled with the two-carat diamond on his left little finger. "Jim, I'm always glad to see you, but I wish you'd quit trying to talk Nelly May into leaving. That woman's my star attraction. She's what pulls them in from the other tents. Why do you want to cause trouble?"

"Amos, you wouldn't understand."

The saloonkeeper shook his head and walked off as Nelly May finished her song. Applause, cheers, whistles filled the tent, and she gave a little bow, then said something to Marv Green.

Jim watched her ankle across the dance floor. She had an hourglass figure, and the black gown was in stark contrast to her creamy flesh. When she reached Jim's table, he stood up. "Can I buy you a drink?"

"That's what I'm here for."

Jim pulled out a chair. When she was seated, he moved it in toward the table, then took the chair across from her. He was keenly aware of her beauty. "Haven't seen you in a couple of days. How are things going?"

"Can't complain, but better now that you're here."

"I wish you meant that."

Her lips smiled, but her eyes stayed the same. "Jim, you know how I feel about you."

"I haven't the faintest notion."

"You're sweet. You treat me like a lady, and I like that."

A waiter stood at the table. Nelly May said, "The usual," and Jim ordered a beer. "I've often wondered. What is the usual?"

"Colored water."

"You mean I'm paying fifty cents for colored water?"

"You're paying fifty cents for my company. I work here, remember. If I drank the real stuff, I wouldn't last till the joint closes."

He took out a cigar, bit off the end, held a match to it. Her eyes stayed directly on him, and he experienced the heavy need, the stirring excitement, the quiet discomfort he always knew when they were together. To cover his emotions, he glanced around the tent. The musicians' break had ended, and they struck up a lively "Oh! Susanna." Men handed dance tickets to white-shouldered, heavily painted women and followed them onto the dance floor. The crowd had turned rowdy now. The sound of voices dashed against canvas walls. Glass tinkled. The ivory balls of the roulette wheel clicked hollowly. Over all the noise rode the funky odor of cheap-perfumed women and sweaty men.

"You don't belong in a place like this," Jim said.

"So you've told me."

"I mean it. You're beautiful. You've got a wonderful voice. Why waste it in this dump?"

"Maybe I ought to be at the Palace in San Francisco."

"Something like that."

"I auditioned at the Palace. They weren't interested. Jim, in San Francisco, I'm just one more pretty face."

"You never told me this before."

"There's lots of things I haven't told you. My job is to provide company, not to talk about my background. Or lack of it."

Jim glanced across the room. This woman was impossible. He couldn't get through to her. She was wasting her life here. He blew a smoke ring but it didn't have a hole in it. Blowing a smoke ring was something else he couldn't do, and he wanted to because Creed did. He admired Creed and wanted to be like him. He looked around. There was Tom Love's sun-bronzed face at one of the poker tables. Farther on, he spotted Arch Wade and, at the bar, a whiskey-smiling Larry Talbot.

The waiter placed the drinks before them, and Jim shelled out seventy-five cents. He looked back at Nelly May, noting how her blond hair curled around her shoulders. Her eyes reminded him of blue diamonds, and her full lips always seemed about to pout. He fought back the desire to pull her close and kiss that mouth. It was a desire he fought every time he was near her.

He sampled his drink. It tasted watery and probably was. Jim felt a sudden annoyance with the drink, the night, and Nelly May. "You ought to get married and raise a family."

"I've had a family. I didn't like it."

"You've been married?"

"I didn't say that. I said I'd had a family. I know what it means to be a wife. No, thank you."

"I don't understand you."

"Why bother?"

"I don't know." He didn't dare tell her the truth. She'd laugh at him.

"Do you want to dance?"

"Am I boring you?"

"If you want to talk, it's my job to listen, but we always cover the same ground. It might be more fun to dance."

Jim laid his cigar in an ashtray and stood up; she followed him to the dance floor, where he purchased five tickets from one of Bullard's flunkies. The band made a waltz out of "Over the Waves," and he twirled her in a one-two-three routine around the floor. Jim was an excellent dancer, and she matched him step for step. He enjoyed the firmness of her body against his, the softness of her cheek against his face, the fragrance of her shoulder-length hair buried against his nostrils. She fitted him as though they were made for each other.

Someone bumped him from the rear. A drunken voice said, "Watch where you're going," and the spell was broken. Jim became aware of the other dancers crowding the floor. Every man held a woman cheek to cheek, chest to breast. Jim halted in mid-step, whirled, and stalked off the floor, dragging Nelly May behind him.

She wrestled her hand from his. "What's wrong? You bought five tickets."

"Keep 'em. You can cash them in later." They had reached the table, and he flung himself into a chair and gulped down the remainder of his beer. Then he reached for his cigar and fired it up.

The waiter appeared at the table and set down two drinks. Jim handed him the cash. Nelly May leaned forward. "You're in a strange mood tonight. Things going badly on the job?"

"The job's fine."

"What about the surveying?"

"Fine. The colonel said when the tracks are laid I'll be ready to hold a surveyor's job. He's going to line me up in San Francisco. With a couple of years' experience, I should be able to start my own business."

"Then what's the problem?"

"You're the problem. You ought to have a dream. When you leave here, you'll end up in some other dump. Don't you ever think of your future?"

"Jim, I make more money in one night than most men make in a month. What do you think I'm doing with that money?"

"That's not the point. You don't belong in a place like this. You're not like the rest of these women."

"I'm exactly like them. I've worked in saloons since I was fifteen. It's all I know. Now why don't you quit trying to run my life? I don't need a big brother."

His cigar had gone out, so he held a match to it. He wondered why he kept punishing himself by coming here. It always ended like this, him angry and her defensive. He was a fool, but he couldn't keep away from her. He'd go off angry tonight and stay away for a couple of days. Then he'd be back asking for more. He'd never be able to get close to her. He didn't think anyone could. That was the tragedy. She was too much woman to go to waste like this.

Nelly May's gaze went beyond the table. Her eyes widened as she tossed down her drink. "I've got to go."

"What do you mean, go? I'm buying drinks, and you can sit here as long as I'm paying."

"She means it's time to join the men."

Jim looked up into Tully Williams's flushed, argumentative face. Tully loomed, wide-shouldered, over the table. His black eyes smoldered, and Jim read the dare in that quarrelsome face. He reached over and pinned Nelly May's arm to the table. "You're with me." Then he glanced around to find the waiter.

Tully placed both hands on his hips. His lips rolled back to reveal clenched teeth. "I told you to keep away from her."

Nelly May tried to reach her feet, but Jim's hand held her in a half-slumped position. "Tully, I get paid to be friendly to people. Jim's a customer."

"You're too friendly with him. I don't like it."

"Jim's just another customer."

Tully's teeth clicked. "I think it's time we settled this."

A smiling Amos Bullard stepped up to

70

Tully. Behind Bullard stood two of his muscular bully boys. "Gentlemen, you know I don't allow violence in the tent. Tully, why don't you move on to the bar."

Tully glared at Bullard, then at Jim. "One of these days you won't have anyone around to take your part. Coming, Nelly May?"

She jerked her arm free of Jim's grasp. "Sure. I've finished my drink here. Thanks, Jim."

Jim churned inside. His right hand rolled into a fist. He felt Bullard squeeze his shoulder. Bullard said, "Want the boys to throw him out?" Jim shook his head. Bullard and the colonel were close. That explained the offer. He didn't want to offend the railroad, and the colonel was the railroad. Damn Bullard! Even Nelly May tried to protect him. When she'd seen Tully, she'd almost choked swallowing that colored water. Hell. He was old enough to look out for himself. After a moment, Bullard shrugged, motioned his men back to their posts, and strolled toward the bar.

The fiddler hit a low note that corresponded with the sinking feeling in Jim's belly. He glanced at the bar, saw Tully with his arm around Nelly May's waist, holding her tightly against him. They were both laughing. Tully glanced in Jim's direction, grinned, and pulled

71

Nelly May even tighter before turning back to the bar. Jim muttered a profanity. He focused on the table. It hurt to see Tully with his hands all over Nelly May. It hurt worse to see her acting as though she enjoyed it.

The opposite chair squeaked, and Jim looked up to find Tom Love watching him. "When are you going to learn to stay away from that woman? She's no good."

"I don't need a lecture, Tom."

"What you need is a new head. That woman's nothing but trouble. None of these women are."

"I don't want to discuss it."

"You'd better do more than discuss it. If you don't stay away from her, sooner or later you're going to have to fight Tully. He's three inches taller than you, and thirty pounds heavier."

"I can take care of myself."

"Tully will eat you alive."

"Let's just drop it."

"It's your neck."

The acrid smell of tobacco reached Jim, and his attention centered on Tom. Tom blew out some smoke, said, "I guess Creed should be at Raton Pass."

"That's what I was telling Charlotte. She's worried."

"If there's one man you don't have to worry

72

about, it's Creed Weatherall."

"That's what I told her."

"Now there's a woman for you. Wait until you get to Frisco, Jim. Get your own business. You'll meet a woman like her then. The kind of woman to raise a family with."

"Charlotte worked in a saloon."

"She ran a gambling table. She didn't hustle drinks or sell her body. Don't try to compare Charlotte Weatherall with Nelly May Scott. Nelly May's no good. Face up to it."

Jim studied the calluses on his palms. His expression sobered; then he lifted his eyes to the bar. He found a vacant spot where Tully and Nelly May had stood, and near the rear of the tent movement caught his attention. He got a glimpse of Tully and Nelly May strolling through the open flap, arms around each other's waists. He went cold inside and he felt the need to hit somebody. He shook his head. Tom was right. He should stay away from Nelly May. The trouble was, he couldn't.

Thunder shook the heavens. Rain pounded the roof. Wind rattled the inn's faded siding. The noise roused Weatherall from sleep, and he sat up on the side of the bed. He was not one of those people who come instantly awake; he dug at his eyes with clenched forefingers, scrubbed his face with his hands. He pushed to his feet, walked to the chamber pot, voided, then resumed his seat on the side of the bed. He pulled out his American Horologe, opened the case, and saw the hands set at six o'clock. Almost night.

The storm seemed to center over the inn. Thunder reverberated off the surrounding peaks. Rain lashed the shingled roof. Wind ripped at the siding. Weatherall stuck a cigar in his teeth, chewed on it. He reviewed all he had seen and heard, searching for some door he could unlock, some opening he could drive through. Walt Clanton hated and feared Rod, but Weatherall saw no way to exploit that relationship. The kid hated and feared Clanton, but again Weatherall drew a blank. Ruby Lee, of course, feared and hated all of them, yet how could she help? He remembered that brief moment when their gazes had locked during dinner. He'd felt then and now that she'd been trying to tell him something. But what?

A heavier rain splattered the roof. The wind howled its fury. Weatherall held a match to the cigar. The smoke burned his broken lips and stung his nostrils. His ribs hurt where O.K. had hit him, and he gingerly fingered the knot that throbbed over his right temple. He'd been a fool. He'd ridden right into the trap O.K. Powell had set for him. It should have been obvious that the rumor he'd heard at Pueblo had been planted. Don Adams, who ran the Colorado, was no idiot. He'd have kept his move on Raton Pass quiet if it hadn't suited his plans to do otherwise.

Weatherall swung to his feet. He'd never liked inactivity, and he'd been locked in this room for hours. O.K. wanted him to sweat. Well, he was sweating. But locking him in a fourteen-foot-by-twelve-foot room wouldn't break him. He stepped over to the boarded-up window. Rain pounded the planks. It seeped between tiny cracks, dribbled down the rough lumber to puddle at his feet.

His mind turned to Charlotte. She'd be at the mess tent now, sharing supper with the colonel, Will Johnson, and Jess Strawberry. The memory of their last night together warmed him like good whiskey. He couldn't believe, wouldn't believe, that their life together was over. They'd experienced too much, yet too little, for it to end now. Somehow a break would happen. He'd make it happen.

He kicked a chair across the room in abrupt frustration. Although it was chilly, perspiration beaded his forehead. He felt anxious. Scared. Desperate. If there was a way out, he couldn't think of it.

A key grated in the lock. The door swung open and Walt Clanton paused on the threshold. He spotted the overturned chair and snickered. "O.K. wants you downstairs, although I don't see why he wastes the grub."

When they reached the table, Weatherall noted that the seating arrangement had changed. O.K. now sat with his back to the fireplace. Rod hunkered at the table's far end. Weatherall sat across from O.K., with the kid to his right. Clanton took the chair at the head of the table. Rain still fell in a driving downpour, but the thunder had ceased. Wind gusted around the inn, rattling the windows. Ruby Lee shuffled in from the kitchen. She set platters of fried beef, hashed potatoes, and bread before them, then returned to the kitchen and brought back two pots of steaming coffee. Then, she slunk into her niche next to the fireplace.

O.K. forked a slice of beef onto his plate, then added two heaping spoonfuls of potatoes. The food rounded the table until everyone had filled his plate. O.K. cut off a chunk of beef, stuck it in his mouth. "Mighty good eating. Ruby Lee's a fine cook. How about the little wife, Creed? Can she cook?"

Weatherall tore a chunk of bread in half, met O.K.'s mirthful gaze. "What difference does it make?"

O.K. chewed his meat in a reflective manner. "They tell me good cooking is the way to a man's heart." He glanced at Clanton, laughed contemptuously. "How about that, Walt?"

Clanton scooped some beef onto his bread. "I can think of other ways."

"I bet you can. No, Creed, from what I've heard, your wife couldn't boil water. But like Walt says, cooking ain't everything."

Weatherall felt his teeth grind together. A sourness filled his throat, his mouth, but he calmly swallowed a mouthful of potatoes. Rain blackened the windows and cascaded off the roof. The kid poured himself a cup of coffee, splashed in some milk. He looked worn out, and wind had reddened his sly face. Rod ate methodically: beef, potatoes, and bread followed by more beef, potatoes, and bread. Weatherall glanced at Ruby Lee, but she kept her head lowered so he couldn't see her eyes.

One lamp sat between Weatherall and O.K. A second flickered in front of the kid. Beyond the lamplight, the room retreated into shadowy darkness. In his mind, Weatherall tried to fit some plan together, but he couldn't formulate anything. They had him boxed in. And despite their relaxed attitudes, they anticipated that he would make a move, and they were ready for it. If it weren't for those supposed ten men in Trinidad, he'd be dead already.

O.K. glanced across the table. "I hear you found your wife in a hell-on-wheels saloon."

"That's right."

"I'm a bit surprised that a man with your high standards would take up with a tent woman."

"Charlotte ran a table."

"Table?"

"She was a gambler."

"If she was a tent woman, whatever gambling she did she did on her back."

Weatherall's teeth clicked together. He kept his eyes on his plate, but his vision blurred. Somehow he managed to jam his fork into a piece of meat. "It worked earlier, O.K. It won't work now."

"Too bad. I was hoping you'd give us an excuse to kick you around."

Clanton's lips curved down inside his wiry growth of beard. "I don't need no excuse."

O.K.'s gaze shifted to Clanton. "Like I said earlier, you can take a crack at him any time you want."

Clanton's head lowered. His fork scraped his plate as O.K. glanced back at Weatherall. At the table's far end Rod snorted, and the kid shifted around nervously. Weatherall kept his attention on the table. He let the location of every object in this room filter through his thoughts: the doors, the windows, the musket behind the bar, the wood box. He could think of nothing that would help him.

Walt Clanton forked the slice of beef from the platter. "Ruby Lee, get us some more meat."

After she picked up the platter and disappeared into the kitchen, O.K. pushed his chair back from the table and refilled his coffee cup. "Creed, I heard you made quite a name for yourself with the Central Pacific. They say the line wouldn't have gone through without you."

"I had no idea you were so interested in me."

"I've kept up. The only reason I didn't join Buck Weaton was that I was making little rocks out of big ones. Soon as I got out I traced you to the Denver line. I got a score to settle."

Ruby Lee broke through the curtains, carrying a tray of meat in her right hand. She set the platter on the table. The rain drove into the inn's wooden shingles. It roiled around rough-hewn eaves. Rod fished out his corncob, stuck it between his teeth, sucked at the empty stem. "Suppose he ain't lying about those men in Trinidad."

O.K. grunted. "One thing's certain. We don't have to worry tonight. Not with this weather."

Rod removed the corncob from his mouth. He stared at Weatherall. "That's my point. We're in here high and dry. The pass is open."

Clanton nodded. "If they left Trinidad early this afternoon, they'd have plenty of time to get here." Clanton slammed his fist down on the table. "He's too damn cool. He ain't worried about nothing."

O.K. adjusted his chair to a more comfortable position. His emerald eyes cut into Weatherall, and two long furrows crinkled his low brow. The kid fingered his mustache, touched his dirty hair. His Adam's apple jumped as his shifty eyes flashed to Weatherall, then back to Rod. Clanton ran a hand down his face. He pulled at his beard, and his teeth showed in a tobacco-stained line.

The kid's reedy voice sounded like an out-of-tune flute. "Maybe we ought to take a look outside."

Shoving the pipe into his vest pocket, Rod stood up. "That's just what I'm going to do." He pushed the kid down as he tried to stand. "Stay here. If we get separated, we're liable to shoot each other." Rod grabbed his hat and a slicker from a nearby stand, and left.

The relaxed atmosphere surrounding the table had disappeared. These men were edgy. They had doubts, and doubts fueled fear. Weatherall's teeth sank into his cigar. The odds weren't good, but he had a feeling this was his best chance. The most dangerous man in the group would be gone for fifteen or twenty minutes.

Weatherall looked up beyond the table to find Ruby Lee. Her eyes were on him, and her lips formed words that he couldn't read. He lowered his head, not wanting Clanton to note this interplay. Weatherall gave Ruby Lee one more short glance, then looked at the lamp, at Clanton, and, lingering, at the woodbox. When he looked up at Ruby Lee, her chin dipped almost imperceptibly.

Weatherall leaned forward. His right hand reached out toward the coffeepot, but when that hand paralleled the oil lamp, he grabbed its base and flung the lamp into Clanton's flannel shirt. As Clanton roared, Weatherall grasped the table with both hands. He drove the table up and over — its edge caught O.K. in the midsection and tipped his chair backward. Weatherall flung the table into the man's sprawled form, then swung around toward the kid, who had jumped to his feet. The kid's revolvers were half out of their holsters, but Weatherall slammed an uppercut into the kid's liver. The kid blanched and froze in place. Weatherall dropped him with a short, chopping left hook to the point of the jaw.

As the kid hit the floor, Weatherall fell to one knee. He ripped the six-gun from the kid's left hand and wheeled back toward Clanton. Blood brightened the side of Clanton's face. Ruby Lee raised a length of blood-stained firewood to strike Clanton but he caught her descending arm and hurled her into the wall. Clanton wheeled around to ward off Weatherall and reached for his pistol. Weatherall raised his six-gun, and squeezed off a round that drilled a hole in Clanton's forehead.

Wood scraped against wood as O.K. shoved the table up on one side and kicked free of its entanglement. Revolver in hand, he pushed up to one knee and fired two rapid shots that whistled so close to Weatherall's ear they startled him. Fighting the panic that clogged his throat, Weatherall lined his sights on O.K.'s chest. He squeezed the trigger and the bullet caught O.K. in the chest, slamming him back into the fireplace.

The acrid smell of cordite, mixed with the grainy odor of burning coal oil, swept over the room. Weatherall edged forward to confirm that O.K. was dead. He watched Ruby Lee step away from the wall to glare down at Clanton. She spat in the man's face and kicked his inert body. Weatherall turned back to the kid, who was out cold. He dragged the kid's second revolver from its holster and stuck both guns in his belt. Two strides carried him to the wall, where he ripped down an Indian blanket. Fire burned a zigzag trail across the center of the house, and Weatherall ran around the table to kick the oil-leaking lamp away from the flames. He tossed the blanket at Ruby Lee, wheeled over to the wood box to tear off a second blanket hanging from the wall. Blanket in hand, he sprang back to the trail of fire.

Ruby Lee screamed and bolted toward the front of the room. Weatherall yelled to her, "Don't go near that door," but she ignored him. She reached the door, yanked it open, and fell backward as two harsh reports boomed outside.

Weatherall cursed. He dropped the Indian blanket and ran over to Ruby Lee's fallen body. His fingers sought the big artery on her neck, but it had ceased to beat. Another pistol shot ripped the night, sending Weatherall scrambling away from the door. He picked up a blanket and quickly beat the fire out. As darkness flooded the room, the smells of coal oil, smoked wool, and charred wood scorched his nostrils. He dropped the blanket and considered his situation. Rod was waiting out front. Apparently he had heard the gunfire and returned to the inn. When Ruby Lee opened the door Rod must have assumed Weatherall was attempting to escape.

Weatherall's teeth clenched. He tried to put himself in Rod's place. Tried to imagine what the man was thinking. He had probably positioned himself close enough to the inn to see anyone slipping through the front door. That route was closed to Weatherall, leaving the back free, with a clear path to the stables. But a horseman couldn't get out of here without cutting around the inn and entering the pass — and Rod was an excellent shot. He'd kill anyone trying to ride out of here.

There'd been five of them, so Weatherall assumed at least six horses were in that stall. He could stampede the bunch, and, with luck, Rod wouldn't be able to pick out the one with a rider.

He felt his way to the curtain and then followed the wall under the staircase until his hand touched the rear door. He opened it carefully and looked out into a blinding downpour. He could see no farther than two feet beyond him. When he stepped through the doorway, his boots struck a stony yard, but the noise couldn't possibly carry over this storm. Wind struck his face. It blew his hair awry, dashed rain against his face. He remembered the position of the corral and headed in that direction until he found a rail fence. Following the fence, he reached the barn. He rounded the corner and found an open door.

His instinct drilled his nerves, and an alkaline taste puckered his mouth. He'd figured wrong. Rod hadn't waited out front: He knew his man needed a horse, so he'd waited inside the barn.

Weatherall pulled one of the revolvers from his belt. He couldn't hoof it out of here. It was half a day's walk to Trinidad. A man without a horse wouldn't have a chance.

Weatherall sidestepped into the building and flattened himself against the wall, waiting for his vision to adjust to the darkness. All his senses keened, and he swore he could hear his own beating heart. His eyes peered through the inky stable. His ears strained. His nostrils flared as some age-old instinct long buried under civilization's thin mantle came alive. The trappings of mankind fell away as the animal in him surfaced.

Letting his gut feelings guide him, he moved along the wall until he reached the first stall. When his hand grasped the door, the horse inside nickered softly as its hooves rustled straw. Weatherall hesitated. He waited for some tell-tale motion in the stable's shifting gloom that would mark Rod's location. Weatherall bit his lip, ignoring the pain from his torn mouth. He edged on to the next stall, groped past the gate until his searching fingers settled on a halter hanging from a nail. When he eased the gate forward, its squeal blasted through the darkness like a steam engine's whistle. Weatherall's heart stopped. Sweat stung his neck and beaded on his face as he waited for Rod's reaction. Nothing. Absolutely nothing. He pushed the gate open and crept into the stall, where his extended hand fell on the trembling animal's neck.

Weatherall stroked the horse's neck and whispered in its ear. He caressed the soft muzzle. Then he wrapped his fingers in the long mane and led the animal out of the stall. He took two quick sidesteps that put him at the horse's rear and slapped the animal hard on the hindquarters. The horse neighed out its fright. Its front hooves thrashed empty air, and it galloped toward the barn's gray-outlined doorway. A red streak flashed at the barn's rear and a gunshot shattered the stillness. Weatherall locked in on that flash. He squeezed the trigger twice and his revolver rocked his hand. He heard a thump, followed by a moan. Then silence.

Horse hooves echoed from beyond the barn. Rain splashed on the arched roof, and wind rattled a loose board on the barn's siding. Uncertain, Weatherall held his position. Rod might be hit. He might be dead . . . or he might be acting. But this couldn't drag on through the night. If Rod were alive, Weatherall didn't want to face him in the daylight. Rod was simply too good. In a shootout, the outcome wasn't even debatable.

Sliding forward a foot at a time, Weatherall reached the third stall. He opened the door, slipped inside to find a neighing, skittish animal backing away from him. He grabbed the horse's mane, pinned the animal into a corner, and talking softly, forced a metal bit into its mouth. He pulled the crownpiece over its head, behind its ears, and led the shivering beast into the runway. Swinging up on the horse's back, Weatherall kicked it in the flanks and, bending low over its back, headed out of the barn in a ground-covering gallop. No shots sounded as he cleared the stable, and he reined the animal left toward the pass with a sigh of relief.

CHAPTER 5

Charlotte Weatherall poured milk into the cup of coffee Colonel Wade Thompson set before her. She stirred the coffee absentmindedly, her green eyes watching the colonel pour himself three fingers of bourbon. Late-afternoon sunlight shifted through the coach's open window. Charlotte's red hair was pinned up, and a breeze cooled the back of her neck. Gray pinstriped pants and a linen shirt clung loosely to her mature figure.

The colonel stuck a Long Nine between his teeth, clamped down on it. "Creed should be back today or tomorrow. He's been gone almost two weeks."

"Too bad he had to make the trip for nothing."

"It is, but two weeks ago we thought we were heading for El Paso and Mexico City. Sure you don't want a shot in that coffee?"

"You know I don't drink. Why are you always trying to corrupt me?"

"There's nobody else, and it's no fun drinking alone. Besides, anyone who smokes cigars should drink. The two go together."

A smile broke the serious planes of Charlotte's face. The colonel was only trying to cheer her up. She was lonely. She missed Creed, and she was a bit more than annoyed that he'd been sent off on a wild-goose chase. She didn't blame the colonel; he took orders like everyone else. But why couldn't General Sheffield have decided to change routes *before* Creed was sent to Raton Pass?

Someone knocked on the door, bringing the colonel to his feet. He strolled across the coach to open the door on Creed Weatherall. The colonel grabbed Weatherall's hand. "Holy cow! We were just talking about you."

Weatherall returned the colonel's handshake, but his eyes were on his wife. Then four swift steps carried him to the table, where he smothered her in his arms. She held him close, fighting back the stinging sensation in her eyes. She so wanted to kiss him but knew he would be embarrassed. After a moment, her head tilted up and she laid a hand on his whiskered cheek. His features looked drawn, and dirt and dust colored his clothing. He smelled like a sweaty mule.

When he stepped away from her, she abruptly noted that he wore no hat and his gunbelt was missing. Two revolvers were thrust in his waistband, but neither of them was his. "What happened to you?"

He gave her his old nothing-to-worry-about grin. "Not much."

"Where's your hat? Your gunbelt?"

"Got lost in a storm. Guess the railroad will have to replace them when I turn in my expense report."

Charlotte took out one of her long, thin cigars and held a match to it. She'd probably never get the truth out of him, but she could tell he had run into trouble. Lots of it. She sank back in her chair, knowing better than to question him. Some things she could push Creed about; others, she couldn't. She had long ago learned to recognize the difference. "You look tired," she said.

"I've been on the trail for almost two weeks."

"Creed, can I fix you a drink?" the colonel asked.

"A stiff one."

Sunlight dimmed across the carpet. The wind freshened. Somewhere out near the corral, metal banged against metal. The colonel handed Weatherall a drink.

Creed hoisted the glass, said, "Here's to being home," and downed half the bourbon.

Voices reached into the coach as men passed on their way to the boarding cars. Charlotte studied her husband. He seemed to fill the coach's small, curtained-off living quarters. Thick black hair fell over his forehead and curled around his ears. Their gazes locked, and in his eyes' gray depths she saw the love he felt for her.

Weatherall pulled out a chair and sat down at the table. "Well, Colonel, the pass is open."

The colonel looked down at his hands. His teeth clamped into his cigar. "Creed, I'm ashamed to have to tell you this, but the trip was for nothing."

"I thought something was wrong when I didn't run into the grading crew or the track-layers. What's up?"

"We're heading in the opposite direction. The El Paso–Mexico City line's off. At least for the time being."

"But why?"

"Money. General Sheffield couldn't find the backers."

"You've got to have money no matter what direction you build."

"True. But if we build up to Leadville, the money is there."

"Leadville? That's mining country."

"Silver. The mountains are full of it. The stockholders want a payoff, and if we build to Leadville, we can give it to them. The general has already got enough backers to cover the tab."

91

"You seem sure it will pay off."

"It's a no-lose proposition. Right now there's twelve hundred teams freighting out of Leadville. They're hauling between ten thousand and fifty thousand pounds of bullion every day."

Weatherall gave a low whistle. He finished his bourbon. "You're sure?"

"You'd better believe it. The freight lines charge eighteen dollars a ton. We can beat that price, and we can move the bullion a lot faster. Once we get there, this line will finally start making money."

Bourbon splashed on the table as the colonel poured himself another drink. He looked at Weatherall and placed the bottle on the table. Charlotte sipped her coffee, then replaced her cup in its saucer. The coffee was too cold.

The colonel dipped his cigar butt in his bourbon. He stuck the cigar in his mouth, sucked at it. "Ever since we left Denver, we've been laying out money with nothing coming in. It's not like it was with the Central Pacific. Then, we could depend on the government. But the government doesn't support the railroad anymore. We only get two hundred feet of right-of-way, plus twenty acres for stations every ten miles. No money."

Weatherall said, "What route are we taking?"

"We'll follow the Arkansas River west to Canon City, then go through the Royal Gorge and swing north along the river to Leadville."

"You're going to put a railroad through the Royal Gorge?"

"We have to."

"Colonel, it can't be done."

"I'm inclined to agree, but that's the route General Sheffield has mapped out."

Charlie saw her husband's head shake. Smoke trickled through her nostrils. "What's so bad about this gorge?"

Weatherall glanced at her. "It's a chasm ten miles long, at least two thousand feet deep, with no room for track at the bottom." He swung back to the colonel. "How do you expect to lay track?"

"The general feels that we can blast out enough rock for a roadbed."

"Colonel, as far as I know there's never been a man who's traversed that entire gorge. Who knows what conditions are down there?"

"It's been traversed. General Sheffield sent a surveying party through there in 'sixty-nine. They marked out a roadbed with paint. All we have to do is grade and make track."

"Glad I'm not the chief engineer."

"You ever see the gorge?"

"Once. About five years ago. All I could see was a thin strip of river down there. That gorge is so deep the sun never hits the bottom. You've got yourself a job, Colonel. How are you going to work it?"

"We'll have a crew at the gorge blasting and grading. We'll work another crew from here to Canon City, and I'll send a third crew to start building from the gorge's far end toward Leadville."

"You'll need more men."

"Jess is on his way to Canon City right now. He'll round up about a hundred pick-and-shovel people for us. I'm sending you to Canon City with supplies."

"Colonel, I just rode in."

"You don't have to leave for a couple of days. Take Charlotte with you. The trip will be good for her."

"How far to Canon City?" Charlotte asked.

"About a hundred miles, but some pretty country between here and there. Take about a week to make it with the wagons."

Weatherall said, "I take it you're going to run this end. What grade are we talking about?"

"Not too bad. We're at four thousand feet here. Canon City sits at a little over five thousand. Equals out to about a thousand foot. Nothing like we had to handle in the Sierras."

"Any bad spots in between?"

"None."

Charlotte glanced at her husband. "One good thing — we won't be fighting the Colorado, so that means you won't have any trouble from Dallas Mason."

The colonel nodded. "That is a break. Now that we're not in competition, there shouldn't be any more dirty tricks. All we have to do is make track."

Charlotte pushed her cup and saucer back. "Colonel, if that's all, I'm going to take Creed down to the mess hall and ask Jake to heat some water. I don't think we can eat supper until Creed gets a bath."

Dallas Mason tucked the bottle of champagne safely under his left arm and glanced down the dirt street that ended at Bullard's Emporium. He'd been in camp eight days and had spent a lot of time in Bullard's tent. Dallas was fond of cards and fond of women. Bullard offered both.

A cool breeze stirred, bringing the fresh scent of pine needles. Lamplight splashed irregular patterns along the street, and a woman's false laugh rang across the night. Rough, tough men walked this street. The wrong look could be dangerous. A careless word could be fatal. Dallas's fingers unconsciously traced the scar on his right cheek. The scar was a remembrance of a shootout at Eagle Lake when he'd worn a deputy sheriff's badge. He'd been eighteen years old and had killed his first man.

His mouth soured with displeasure as his gaze probed the street. He was sick of towns like this, sick of the kind of job he'd come here to do. But it was all he knew. He'd lived by the gun since he was sixteen years old and rode shotgun for the El Paso Stage Line. From shotgun guard, he'd graduated to deputy sheriff, then at nineteen to town marshal, and at age twenty he'd reached the peak of his profession when he'd been appointed a U.S. deputy marshal.

By then he'd earned a reputation as a man not to tangle with. He was hard-nosed, afraid of nothing, and proud of it. Guns had always been a part of his life. He'd been raised by his father, who had run El Paso's livery stable. (His mother had died during childbirth.) His father, an avid hunter, had given Dallas his first rifle when the boy was five. Dallas was a crack shot by the time he was eight, but it was the handgun that fascinated him. The first time he'd held a revolver in his hand, it had become an extension of his arm. All he had to do was point, squeeze the trigger, and he hit the target. He was a natural.

He had enjoyed wearing the star. It made him feel important. The law was everything, and he was never above using unconventional methods to enforce it. He'd been a hard-working lawman: honest, impartial, completely self-reliant. But because of his unconventional methods, he'd had problems with his superiors from the beginning. And he was hot-tempered, impetuous, and overly ambitious. These last traits had been his undoing, and after twelve years with the U.S. marshal's office, he'd made a mistake that had ended his career.

The firing had devastated him. He'd been proud of his job, proud of his ability to perform it. He couldn't go back to being a town marshal or deputy sheriff. His pride wouldn't allow it. He couldn't run a livery stable for the same reason. He'd tried prospecting, but it was a hard, lonely life. He hadn't been able to find anything that gave him satisfaction. The loss of his badge and the authority that went with it had reduced him to a nothing. Then he'd heard about a problem near Casper, Wyoming. Cattle rustling was wiping out the established ranchers, and local lawmen were powerless. Everyone knew who was responsible, but not enough evidence could be found to make a case. It had been a clear-cut instance of wrong versus right. For a fee, he'd offered to resolve the situation. After that incident, offers just seemed to come his way, so he'd drifted into the role of enforcer.

He'd always told himself that he represented the right side. He had a code, and he lived by it. He always gave his opponents a chance to pull out, and if they didn't, he always faced them head-on. Yet, standing here tonight, he understood his life had been a lie. He'd always worked for the right side because he would convince himself that whoever hired him was on the right side. In fact, he worked for whatever side came up with the money.

When he'd arrived here to find that Creed Weatherall was troubleshooter for the Denver Railroad, he'd been dismayed. Although Dallas hadn't seen him in six years, Creed was one of the few friends he'd ever had. He didn't want to have to kill Creed Weatherall. He would have quit, but to do so would have ruined him. Word would get out that he was undependable. Or even worse, afraid. It would be difficult to find work, and every young gunslinger looking for a reputation would be eager to take him on. Suddenly he was sick of it all. Why couldn't he have followed in Creed's tracks? When Creed had been fired, he'd found a decent job. He'd established a new career. He was even married. He lived the kind of life that those men who occupied the gray fringe between right and wrong could only imagine.

Dallas shook his head. It was too late to change now. A drunken railroader bumped into him. The man gave him a hard stare, then stumbled on. Dallas swung around to face the railroad yard. He had avoided Creed since arriving in camp, but tonight he planned to renew their friendship. He had not wanted to see Creed because it had seemed a showdown loomed between them. Now, thanks to a change in the Colorado's plans, that showdown wouldn't occur. The two lines would be following different routes, so competition had been eliminated.

He hiked over to the track, circled the work train, and followed the rails until he came to Weatherall's coach. He knocked on the door, waited until it swung open to reveal Creed. Dallas stuck out his hand. "It's good to see you."

Surprise crinkled Weatherall's forehead. Then a smile cracked his lips. He grabbed Dallas's hand, shook it. "I wondered when you'd drop by." Weatherall stepped back, motioned Dallas inside. "Charlotte, I want you to meet someone."

Dallas watched a red-haired, green-eyed woman advance to meet him. She was dressed in a man's trousers and a man's shirt, and a cautious expression veiled her beautiful face.

"Dallas, this is my wife. Charlotte, this is . . ."

"I know who it is."

"Nice to meet you, Missus Weatherall."

"Call me Charlotte."

"Fine. Oh, Creed, I brought a bottle of champagne to celebrate the occasion."

"I didn't think you drank."

"I don't. But I'll hoist one glass to toast the bride. I'm glad things have turned out so well for you."

"They've done that. How are things with you?"

"All right. I wonder sometimes if life's not kind of laid out for you, anyway."

"Sit down. Charlotte, get us some glasses so I can uncork this bottle of champagne. How long you been in camp?"

"About two weeks."

"Were you part of that Raton Pass deal?"

"I don't know what you're talking about."

"I ran into O.K. Powell and some friends down there."

Dallas's lips pursed as Charlotte set the glasses on the table. "You mean trouble?"

"You could say that."

"That's not my way, Creed. I'm surprised you'd ask."

"It didn't use to be, but I had to know if things had changed."

Weatherall peeled the foil from the bottle and popped the cork; as champagne bubbled over the rim, Weatherall tilted it into a glass. He filled the other two and handed one to Dallas, one to Charlotte.

Dallas lifted his glass. "To a long, happy life."

Charlotte said, "That's all I want," and the three of them sipped the bubbly.

Weatherall lit a cigar, leaned back in his chair. "Why did it take you so long to look us up?"

"We were good friends, Creed, but it's been a while. Until today, I didn't know what the future held."

"What changed, then?"

"We're not headed south anymore. We'll swing west, then north. Someplace called Leadville."

Dallas saw that Weatherall and Charlotte looked shocked. Weatherall seemed to settle deeper in his chair, and two lines cut his cheeks when his lips compressed. Charlotte took out a thin cigar, held a match to it. She shook out the match, her gaze dropping to the table. Weatherall removed the cigar from his mouth. "I thought the Colorado was headed for El Paso, then Mexico City. What happened?"

"The line ran out of money. It seems there's

lots of silver in Leadville. Adams can get backers for a line there because it promises a quick payoff. It's not all bad. At least you and I aren't on opposite sides of the fence."

"I'm afraid we are. We're headed for Leadville, too."

Dallas grunted. He fingered the scar on his cheek. "We're right back where we started," he murmured, more to himself than to Weatherall.

"I don't see any problem. This has been a dirty-tricks affair for some time anyway. You slow up my progress. I slow up yours. There's no reason for gunplay."

Dallas's hands squeezed tightly. He looked at Weatherall. "You know better than that. We're talking big money. Somebody has to lose for somebody else to win. Adams is prepared to do whatever it takes."

Weatherall's eyes shifted in Charlotte's direction, then back to Dallas. "We've been friends a long time. We can work something out."

Dallas nodded. "You know, I think you're right." If Creed wanted to protect the little woman from the truth, fine. That was understandable. But they both knew that if it came down to win or lose, it was their job to settle it. That's what they were paid for.

Charlotte fidgeted in her chair, and her right

hand accidentally knocked over her glass of champagne. She leaped up, hurried over to a basket, and returned with a cloth to wipe up the mess. When she sat down, her hand trembled as she brought her cigar to her lips.

An owl hooted in a nearby thicket, and the Arkansas River flowed east with its low murmur. Dallas crossed and recrossed his legs. He felt Charlotte's gaze but refused to look at her. He'd made a mistake coming here. He had the same old high regard for Creed, and, from what he'd seen, he liked Creed's wife. None of this was going to make his job easier.

Charlotte got to her feet. "I've got some sewing to do. I'll let you two talk over old times."

As she disappeared into the sleeping quarters, Dallas drained his glass. The woman didn't like him, and she certainly feared him because she could foresee the future as clearly as he. It was only natural that she should dislike anyone who threatened her husband. Dallas knew he owed Creed as much as one man could owe another. He wouldn't be alive today if it weren't for Creed Weatherall. The knowledge that they probably faced a showdown burned Dallas's gut like turpentine soaking a raw wound.

Weatherall refilled his champagne glass. "What happened in Tucson? Why did you lose your badge?"

"A mistake or, as the government called it, poor judgment. A local tough murdered a woman. He later wounded the town marshal when the marshal tried to arrest him. I found the guy at a bar, but he wanted to make a fight of it. I say he reached for his gun. Onlookers say I didn't give him a chance. Well, you remember. I was always in a jam with the brass. They thought I was a bit too enthusiastic."

"I'm sorry about the job. I know what it meant to you."

"What happened to you?"

"More or less the same thing. Only I killed the wrong man."

"Too bad. But those things happen. At least it worked out for you. You've found a good job and married a fine woman. Maybe it was for the best."

"Killing an innocent man is never for the best. It does something to you inside."

Dallas nodded and looked at the floor. He'd made a bad mistake coming here, and he couldn't afford such mistakes. He was thinking of Creed as a man. In Dallas's business, Creed had to be an object, an obstacle to be overcome. Dallas pushed to his feet. He gave Creed a moody glance. "Getting late. I've got a long day."

"Thanks for dropping by. Too bad you can't stick around. We could play some dominoes."

"Yeah. Like old times . . . Well, be seeing you."

As Weatherall opened the door, Dallas clapped on his hat and stepped into the night.

CHAPTER 6

The nine o'clock sun brightened the foreground. This was the second day that the twelve-person, six-wagon supply train had been on the trail, and Weatherall was pleased with their progress. It was easy going, with plenty of meadowland. Other areas were thinly forested with piñon and juniper, and the trail they broke now led through a thin carpet of prairie grasses.

Weatherall glanced back at the other wagons, their brown canvas tops whitened with trail dust. The colonel had provided him with a dependable crew, but he wished Tully Williams hadn't been included. Tully was a hard worker and a top hand with mules, but he was also a bully who didn't like young Jim Smith. The two men had exchanged angry words several times already. It would be a miracle if the train reached Canon City without those two getting into a fight.

Weatherall shook his head as he clucked his team ahead. What riled the two men was none of his business, so he couldn't interfere. Still, he dreaded the thought of them tangling. Tully was too big, too experienced. He'd beat Jim to a pulp. Weatherall liked Jim. They'd known each other since working the Central Pacific line up to Promontory Point. Jim was a decent, dependable young man, but a bit naive. He should never have gotten involved with Nelly May Scott.

Weatherall felt Charlotte's hand tighten on his leg, and he glanced over at her. She flashed him a smile before her attention turned back to the countryside. "Creed, this is beautiful."

He grunted his agreement. He'd never felt better. He would have been content to drive along like this with his wife beside him for the rest of his life. All those years alone and lonely, and he'd never even realized it. Now he couldn't imagine a day without Charlotte. At times, his newfound happiness frightened him. Life was so transitory.

"I'm glad the colonel let me come along."

"That makes two of us."

"This reminds me of the time in Reno when we had to go back to the mountains for wood. Remember?"

"That was quite a trip."

"I guess that was when I first began to notice you."

"I learned some things about you, too."

"Like what?"

"You're hardheaded. Not too good at following orders."

"Is that all?"

"Oh, no. I learned you could ride like a bronco buster and shoot like Jesse James."

"You sound impressed."

"I am. You're one hell of a woman, Missus Weatherall."

"You're one hell of a man."

"Do you ever miss Jack?"

"I think of him sometimes. He was a good man. A good husband. But that's in the past. I have you now. Sometimes I wonder if you know how much you mean to me."

"I think so. I feel the same way."

"Sometimes I'm so happy it scares me."

"We got a lot of life ahead of us."

Axles squeaked as the land tilted when the wagon rolled through a buffalo wallow to hit an uphill climb. The sun shone directly on them now, and a gentle breeze ruffled Charlotte's red hair. The supply train broke through a stand of pine. Mule hooves clip-clopped around them, and the clean, sweet scent of pine needles washed them in nature's perfume.

Sunlight formed patterns of light and dark on the mules' sweaty backs. The Arkansas River sparkled in the distance. The wagon jolted over the deep tracks of an old south-north road headed toward a stand of juniper that broke the horizon. Wheels groaned, axles whined, singletrees jangled as the four-mule team strained forward.

A match flared. The sour smell of tobacco touched Weatherall's nostrils as Charlotte lit one of her thin cigars. "This seat's getting hard."

Weatherall checked his timepiece. "I'm tired too, but Dallas did us a favor telling us that Adams meant to swing toward the gorge. This time we've got the jump on them."

"It's a race, isn't it?"

"That's right. There's room for only one grade through that gorge. Whoever gets it, gets Leadville."

"Do you think Dallas will resent your using his information?"

"That's the game. Besides, I gave him the information that we're making track to Leadville. They're trying to move out — we just got the jump on them."

"Creed, I think things are going to get worse between the Denver and the Colorado. I'm afraid things will get the way they were at the Central Pacific. I don't want to think about gunplay."

"There's not going to be any. Just more dirty tricks like us pulling out early."

"Don't lie to me. They didn't bring in

Dallas to tear up railroad track and ties."

"Dallas and I have known each other a long time. We can work something out."

"You never did tell me what happened at Raton Pass, but I know it was bad. There's no way you would have given up that Stetson without a fight. And what about your gun-belt?"

"I told you there was a storm. Now forget it."

"I wish I could."

Two hours later, Weatherall drew rein at a grassy spot near the river. The five other rigs pulled in behind them, and everyone piled off the wagons to stretch. A light breeze cooled the plateau as the noon sun shone directly down on them. A stand of piñon ran off to the right, and the mellow call of a wren sounded from the trees.

Charlotte released a sigh. "It's good to get off that seat for a few minutes."

"Yes, ma'am, it sure is," Tom Love said as he hoofed up beside her.

Weatherall lifted a canteen to his lips and swallowed warm water. He recorked the canteen, stuck it back under the wagon box. "Jim, gather up some wood to get a fire going. We'll make some coffee. The rest of you men water these mules. We're going to make this a short stop. By now Dallas Mason must know we're on our way to Canon City. We've got to hold the lead."

Weatherall stared back to the east as the men broke into action. They couldn't have left the main camp without word getting back to the Colorado people, even if they had left in the dark. And the minute Dallas got the news, he'd work up his own train. Weatherall's brow contracted. The tip of his tongue touched his upper teeth. A supply train couldn't catch up with this outfit, but men on horseback could. That gorge was the key that opened the door to Leadville. The Colorado line couldn't let the Denver get there first. Dallas would have to stop these wagons.

As Jim Smith dropped a load of wood to the ground and started a fire, Weatherall quickly evaluated his men. Jim was young, but he was steady. Tom could be depended on. Tully was a blowhard, but he'd probably hold up in a fight. Being a new man, Ace Benson was an unknown quantity. So were Ron Dees, Larry Simpson, and Bruce Waite. Joe Yates, Dell Nelson, George Duncan, and Lee Keene were seasoned railroaders. They would stand their ground. Then there was Charlotte. She was a crack shot and had an iron backbone. Still, he'd made a mistake in bringing her. If things went wrong, she could get hurt.

He believed Dallas didn't want bloodshed any more than he did. But both railroads had millions at stake. Neither one would go down without a fight. Raton Pass had proved that. He hadn't wanted to admit that he and Dallas might have to face each other, but he couldn't deny it any longer.

Charlotte touched his arm. "What's bothering you?"

"Just unwinding."

By now the piñon-wood fire crackled, and Tom Love set a heavy, sooty coffeepot on the flames. The meal consisted of cold beans and cold biscuits washed down with hot coffee. For dessert, they opened several airtights filled with peaches. Tully Williams, grumpy, poured himself a second cup of coffee, leaned against one of the wagons, and watched Jim Smith go to the river to wash his tin plate.

Ace Benson packed his pipe. "I like this country. Should be an easy job grading into Canon City."

A rail-thin Joe Yates nodded. "Looks easy to me. All we have to do is follow the river."

George Duncan stroked his spade-shaped beard. "Thank God we won't have to tunnel. I hate tunneling."

Lee Keene cleared his throat. "That's dangerous business, all right."

Ace puffed on his pipe. "Remember those

thirteen tunnels . . . ."

Weatherall turned to look across the river. Conversation buzzed in the background, but he only half heard it. Charlotte stepped up beside him, and he glanced down at her. She had pushed her broad-brimmed hat back on her head, and midday sun drenched her face. She had to be tired, but fatigue had failed to dull her beauty. She looked trim and fresh, and Weatherall realized anew how much she had become a part of him.

"Creed, something's bothering you."

He shook his head, but Charlotte knew him too well. He'd never be able to hide anything from her.

"Dallas is going to try to stop us, isn't he?"

"Woman, sometimes you're too perceptive. But we've got a head start. We can make good time in this country. Even with wagons." When she started to reply, he held up his hand. "Let's get some more coffee."

They moved over to the fire, where Weatherall refilled their cups. Then he and Charlotte edged away and stood with their backs to the river. Joe Yates cut off a chunk of tobacco and offered the plug to Ron Dees, who held up a protesting hand. The small fire had turned to hot coals that began to break into yellow ashes. To the north a flock of magpies speckled the sky. Chains jingled as the mules moved around restlessly.

Weatherall watched Tom Love amble over to the river to wash his utensils. Tom was one of those lucky individuals who had a way of making everyone like him instantly. It was a character trait Weatherall envied and one few people had. He saw Tully Williams hike toward the dying fire. Tully's arrogant face wore a truculent expression, and his gaze was on young Jim Smith, who stood between him and the fire.

When Tully reached Smith, he deliberately brought his left boot down hard on Smith's instep and without breaking stride marched ahead. Weatherall saw the youngster's cheeks redden. The other men had seen the byplay and stood in embarrassed silence. After Tully had refilled his cup, he tromped back toward Smith. When Tully reached him, he stomped down on Smith's foot again, and again he clumped by. Smith swore and shook off the pain before going after Tully.

Tully reached his wagon, where he swung around to face Smith. A huge grin pulled at Tully's lips as sly anticipation narrowed his eyes.

Weatherall immediately shoved his coffee cup at Charlotte and trotted over to young Smith. "Jim, I want you and Tom to move your wagon up to the lead spot. I'll drop to

114

the rear." Before Smith could reply, Weatherall turned around to the other men. "Let's get ready to move. Ron, kill that fire while Charlotte rinses out the coffeepot."

Charlotte carried the coffeepot to the river and Ron Dees started kicking dirt onto the smoldering embers. Weatherall wheeled toward Tully. "What's between Jim and you is your business, but this trip is railroad business. I don't want any more nonsense."

Weatherall swung away without even taking time to read Tully's expression. He hiked up the line of wagons until he reached his own. By then, Charlotte had washed the coffeepot and stored it away. As she climbed into her seat, Weatherall waved his arms and the wagons clattered ahead. When George Duncan drove the fifth wagon by, Weatherall joined Charlotte and swung his team in line.

She pulled her hat low on her head so that the brim shaded her face. "What did you tell Tully?"

"I asked him to be nice to Jim."

"Think he will?"

"I hope so."

Charlotte chuckled. "Those two are headed for trouble, aren't they?"

"Looks like it."

"Jim must be crazy. That woman can't be worth going head to head with Tully."

"You ever see her?"

"No. Is she that pretty?"

"Almost as pretty as you."

Charlotte threw him an impish grin. "Well, maybe she *is* worth it."

The tableland ran monotonously before them. To their left, sunlight reflected off the Arkansas's eastward-breaking current, and the heavily loaded wagons scarred the yellow-brown earth with deep tracks. Blue sky stretched over them, and a gentle breeze cooled the sweating mules. The clip-clop of hooves lifted and fell in four-beat rhythm as the creak and groan of overloaded wagons drifted across the land.

Two o'clock found them rolling westward over a grassy, flowered plain. Prairie lilies grew here. Prairie snowball and sand begonia dotted the range. The wagons bounced through buffalo wallows, and the mules strained against the slowly rising terrain.

Charlotte reached under the seat to pull out a bag of biscuits. "You want one?" When Weatherall shook his head, she took out a biscuit and shoved the bag beneath the seat. "You seem mighty interested in what might be behind us."

Weatherall grunted, flicked the reins.

"You think Dallas will catch up today?"

"Today or tomorrow."

"What are you going to do?"

"I don't know."

"Why do you keep evading me? We're in for a fight."

"Oh, hell, Charlotte. Dallas and I go back a long way. We've always been on the same side."

"That doesn't change anything. He has to stop these supplies."

"I guess so. Well, we'll handle it when it arrives."

The train edged its way west, following the river. The surrounding prairie grass was spotted with juniper and clumps of stunted piñon. Wagon wheels flattened grayish saltbrush and rolled over prickly pear. As their wagon rattled past a ten-foot juniper, Weatherall reached out to break off a branch and hand it to Charlotte so that she could smell the heady odor.

Glancing back down the side of his wagon, Weatherall saw dust clouds to the east. He glanced at Charlotte and said, "Dallas is right behind us," and as alarm tightened her cheeks, he swung his team around the wagon fronting them and lashed his mules into a run. When he reached the lead wagon, he stood up and signaled the train to stop. Drivers drew rein. Wheels locked. Wagons shuddered to a halt. Weatherall jumped down and jogged along the line of wagons, telling each driver to work his rig into a circle with its back close to the river. As the wagons circled, Weatherall regained his seat and fell into the last spot in line.

After they were in position Weatherall wrapped his reins around the brake handle and leaped to the ground. He stood with hands on hips, gazing eastward. "You men unhitch these mules. Tom, you and Jim take the animals about a quarter-mile upstream and tender them in a buffalo wallow. Then hustle back here. We've got company."

Concern clouded Jim's boyish face. Tom Love nervously stroked his mustache. Ace folded his hands over his protruding belly, his chubby face creased. Tully Williams untied his neckerchief and wiped his brow. His back was straight and tense, and for once his usual belligerent attitude was missing.

Joe Yates cut off a chew of tobacco, shoved it between clenched teeth. Larry Simpson's hand trembled as he held a match to his pipe, and Dell Nelson chewed a cigar to bits. Only George Duncan and Lee Keene seemed unaffected. The two old dynamite hands leaned back against their wagons, arms crossed over their chests. Charlotte stood by Weatherall, her right hand clutching his arm.

Weatherall glanced over at Tom and Jim.

"Let's get those mules moving. The rest of you pull these wagons close together."

Soon after Jim and Tom had returned from securing the mules, Dallas's riders drew rein about fifty yards out from the forted wagons. Weatherall counted sixteen men, and remembering what he'd encountered at Raton Pass, assumed that at least three or four of them would be hard cases, not railroaders. That gave Dallas an edge, but his people were in the open, where there was little cover.

After a moment, Dallas wheeled back to his crew, said something, then kneed his roan toward the circled wagons. He pulled up when he fronted the spot where Weatherall and Charlotte waited. Dallas removed his hat. "Afternoon, Missus Weatherall. I wasn't expecting to find you here. Creed, you're making good time."

"We should cover twenty miles before dark."

Dallas glanced over at Charlotte, then put his gray gaze directly on Weatherall. "Creed, this is the end of the line. I want you to turn those wagons around."

"I can't do that."

"You know I can't let you reach Canon City."

"Then I'd say you've got a problem."

Dallas cleared his throat. He pulled at his

nose, glanced back at the waiting horsemen. Then he faced Weatherall, lips tight, eyes lidded. Behind Weatherall, the Denver men shifted around uncertainly. A subdued muttering broke the silence, and a muted "Damn" reached Weatherall's ears. Dallas dropped from the roan. He walked up to where Weatherall waited and, planting both feet wide, stood with one hand touching a wagon. "Creed, I don't want a fight. You're the best friend I ever had. Be reasonable. You've got nothing tied up in this railroad. So the Colorado reaches the Royal Gorge first. It doesn't cost you anything."

"So the Colorado reaches it last. You've got nothing tied up either."

"I've got my reputation."

"So have I."

"It's not the same thing and you know it. You can go on to another job. But if I back off, you know what happens."

"I know and I'm sorry. But the colonel gave me a second chance and I can't let him down."

Dallas glanced at Charlotte. "Missus Weatherall, can't you talk some sense into him?"

"Not when his mind's made up."

Dallas regarded the individuals ranked behind Weatherall. "Men, I want you to listen

120

to me. You came here to work, not fight. I'm sure some of you have women and children. Do you want to die for a lousy three bucks a day, or do you want to keep supporting your families?"

Weatherall crowded against Dallas, cutting him off from the others. "Quit trying to work around me. I make the decisions here."

Dallas stepped back from Weatherall to where he could give each man a direct look. "I'm going to hold off until morning. Give you a chance to think this over. Try to face facts. This freight isn't going to move another foot unless it moves east."

Weatherall watched as Dallas clapped on his Stetson and remounted the roan. Dallas gave Weatherall one long, pleading gaze, then reined the mount toward his waiting followers.

Weatherall heeled around to his crew. He lit a cigar as the silence dragged out. Charlotte aligned herself beside him.

The men glanced around uncomfortably. They looked at their hands, their feet, the sky. They didn't look at Weatherall.

His tongue arched a smoke ring that floated lazily in the thin air. He knew what they were thinking, and Dallas was right. They were not fighting men, and they didn't get fighting wages. But Weatherall understood that he owed the colonel a debt. So did they.

Jim Smith lit a cigar. His lips rounded to emit a smoke ring that escaped as a solid blob. Tom Love stood with his thumbs hooked in his waistband and gave Weatherall a supportive wink. Lee Keene busied himself with a dip of snuff, his dark, taciturn visage as bland as polished leather. Somebody cleared his throat, and Joe Yates dug a hole in the yellowish topsoil with the toe of one boot.

A magpie's screech in a nearby clump of juniper brought the men out of their introspection. Ace Benson scratched his protruding belly. His moon face reflected his concern. "Creed, I've got a wife and three kids. Nothing was said about anything like this when we left camp."

A squat-figured Joe Yates spewed out a stream of brown tobacco. "The colonel didn't even mention the Colorado was going to build this way."

Weatherall removed the cigar from his teeth. "Don't blame the colonel. I set this up. I thought we could clear camp without Dallas knowing about it."

"Well, you thought wrong," Tully Williams remarked. "You've put us in a hard spot. You know that, don't you?"

Weatherall threw Tully a disgusted glance. "Ever since you've joined this outfit, you've been spoiling for trouble. Now you've found it, so stop whining."

Tully's face turned the color of sunset and his meaty lips pulled together, but his gaze fell away.

Chunky, bald Larry Simpson grasped his suspenders with both hands. He sucked at his empty pipe. "I think we ought to head back to camp. Like Mason said, we're railroad men."

George Duncan pushed his cap back from his forehead. Deep lines drove down his usually placid face. "I think we ought to shut up and listen to Creed. We're getting paid to do a job, not make decisions."

Lee Keene nodded. "Makes sense to me. What do you want to do, Creed?"

"I want to head back for camp just like the rest of you. But we can't. The colonel's counting on us to get this load through. If we don't, the railroad's in trouble. This is a clear case of right and wrong — and a man ought to know the difference."

"What about Charlotte?" Jim said.

"That's no problem," Weatherall replied. "I know Dallas. He'll let her ride out before trouble starts."

Charlotte swung around in front of Weatherall. She put her hands on her hips. "I'm not riding anywhere. I can shoot as well as any man here. Better than most."

123

Weatherall's eyes rolled back. An exasperated sigh broke from his lips. "We'll talk about it later."

"There's nothing to talk about. I'm staying."

The men glanced uneasily at each other, then settled into a thoughtful silence. Tully Williams pulled his railroad cap low over his eyes as his truculent features squared angrily. Jim Smith's easygoing expression turned serious. Tom Love tapped out his pipe and moved over so that he stood near Weatherall. Dell Nelson's face showed a wary uncertainty. Joe Yates sucked on his chewing tobacco, his bulky body frozen with tension.

Ace Benson removed the empty pipe from his mouth. He crossed railroad-tie-sized arms over his chest. "I say we put it to a vote. Everybody's neck's on the line."

"I'm all for that," Ron Dees mumbled.

"Sounds like a good idea," Larry Simpson echoed.

Weatherall drew on his cigar. He studied the ground near the toe of his boot. He didn't like the idea of a vote. There was too big a chance it might go against him. Still, if these men refused to fight, he couldn't make them. And they had themselves to think about. Many, like Ace, had families. "All right. We'll vote. How many want to go back to camp?"

Hands shot up: Tully, Ace, Ron, Joe, Larry, and Dell. That made six voting to go, six voting to stay. Weatherall shrugged. "Well, that didn't solve anything."

Tully leaned aggressively forward. "You said Charlotte rides out. That means she has no vote. It's six to five."

Smoke escaped from Weatherall's nostrils. His gaze locked with Tully's. "I say she has a vote. Look, we're well forted up here. Dallas and his people have no protection out there. Look at the country between us. We can win this fight."

When Jim, George, Bruce Waite, and Lee Keene stepped forward to form a line to Weatherall's left, Tully's lips jerked in a short grimace, but he swung away and tromped over to the circled wagons' far side. In a moment, the other dissenters turned away too.

"I guess that settles that," Lee said.

Dallas Mason gazed into the campfire's yellow-red embers. He sat like an Indian, with his legs tucked under him; his thoughts were on the encircled wagons. The moon's full circle illuminated the prairie, and it was almost as light as that last gray moment before sunrise. Dallas looked down at the length of pine in his left hand. He had passed the time carving, and the soft pinewood was the shape of a crude bowie knife.

An owl hooted from a stand of juniper off to Dallas's right. It was a throaty sound, floating a lonely echo over the flatland. Dallas tossed the pine knife into the fire. He stood up and stared at Weatherall's wagons. He knew Weatherall wouldn't back off. Weatherall would fight, but he wouldn't win. Dallas was certain of that. Nevertheless, it was a fight Dallas didn't want.

Dallas cursed under his breath. His fingers traced the old bullet wound puckering his cheek. A man did what he had to do, but that didn't mean he had to like it. He glanced at the sprawled forms of sleeping men. Most of them were railroaders; however, he'd picked up four roughnecks before leaving Pueblo. They would make the difference tomorrow. Easing over to the fire, he knelt down and poured himself a cup of coffee. Strange how life had a way of moving in circles. When he'd been fired from his job as a U.S. marshal and taken up the gun, he'd never dreamed he'd someday face Creed Weatherall. Creed was like a younger brother, and if one man could love another Dallas loved Creed.

Suddenly Dallas wanted to hurl his cup of coffee across the distance, leap on his roan, and ride until the animal dropped. But that course wasn't open to him. At that moment he envied Weatherall. Since coming here, seeing Creed again, Dallas had abruptly recognized what an empty life he'd led, and only that same emptiness lay before him. He could never have a wife, a family, friends. Wherever he went, his reputation would follow. He couldn't ask a woman to share his life, and, as for friends — who could he trust?

The coffee was fresh-brewed, yet it tasted stale, bitter. He dashed it to the ground, dropped the tin cup, and got to his feet. He gazed off at nothing, his mind caught in the problem he'd face come morning. He couldn't allow those wagons to go west, but he couldn't allow gunplay either. There had to be another way. He had until daybreak to find it.

Sunlight radiated over the prairie. It dried the morning dew and lifted the night's dank chill. Dallas's roan trotted up to the circled wagons, and Weatherall stepped out to meet him. Weatherall's pink-streaked eyes said he hadn't slept either, while behind him the Denver's weary crew grouped in morose silence. Dallas removed his hat. "Morning, Missus Weatherall. Time to start back to camp, Creed."

"You know I can't do that."

"Afraid you'll have to. I've got a couple of men with your mules. If you don't give me your word you'll backtrack, they'll shoot 'em. Be a waste to kill those animals."

Weatherall's head tipped up, then down. He took a cigar from his vest pocket, lit it. "It looks like you've got me."

"I'd say so. A lot better than somebody getting killed, though."

"All right. You've got my word."

"Good enough. See you back at camp." With that, Dallas reined around and trotted the roan back to his own men. Thank God he'd thought of those mules. Otherwise, this place would have been a slaughter ground. He'd known Creed wouldn't budge, but the mules had solved everything. The way this had ended lifted a weight from Dallas's shoulders. Sure, he and Creed would clash again. Every time they did meant finding a way to avoid a showdown. He owed Creed too much to let these two railroads cause a killing.

CHAPTER 7

As the wagons rolled into main camp, Weatherall saw Colonel Thompson striding out from his coach to meet them. Surprise marked the colonel's pudgy features, and Weatherall knew his gray-haired boss was concerned. The colonel was a worrier by nature and seeing these wagons back in camp was something to worry about.

When the wagons creaked to a stop at the main corral, Weatherall jumped to the ground and handed his reins to Hank Storm, who had ambled out to greet them. The other drivers climbed down from their wagons to wait in flinty silence. The sun hit Weatherall in the face as he stared west, and the scent of piñon drifted with the breeze. Charlotte stepped up by Weatherall and told him she was going home to wash up.

Seconds later the colonel confronted Weatherall. "Looks like you had trouble."

"More than we could handle."

"Anybody hurt?"

"No."

"You mean you tangled with Dallas Mason and nobody got killed?"

"Wasn't a shot fired. He told me to turn back or he'd shoot the mules."

"Holy cow! I never figured that for his way."

Weatherall bit the end off a cigar, held a match to it. He was tired, and not just from bouncing around on a wagon seat for two days and missing a night's sleep. He felt guilty about letting the colonel down. He understood there wasn't one thing he could have done, but his failure rankled him. No matter how you sliced the bacon, the colonel had depended on him and he'd failed.

The colonel glanced at the waiting drivers. "You men get some food and rest. Hank will get a crew to take care of the wagons." Then the colonel lit his own cigar, stared off into the distance.

A mule snorted. Bits jangled as metal reflected sunlight across the compound. Beyond the corral lay heaps of wire, kegs of railroad spikes, stacks of ties, and piles of narrow-gauge rail. Weatherall spat out a fleck of tobacco. "I'm sorry we didn't make it, Colonel."

"So am I. It means Adams will beat us to Canon City."

"Maybe that's not too important. The key to building this railroad is the Royal Gorge, not Canon City."

"Meaning?"

"We have to telegraph Jess Strawberry. Tell him to hire some fighting men and fort up that gorge. He'll have to hold until we get there."

"That could take a couple of months."

"We have no choice. The gorge shouldn't be hard to defend. It's rough country, and in some places there's no room for anything but the Arkansas River. All Jess has to do is find a pinhole and block it off."

Despair lined the colonel's cheeks. He pushed a hand through his gray hair. "I didn't want it to come to this. It's the Central Pacific all over again. Holy cow. All I want to do is build a railroad."

"It's fight or pack up."

"I'll get the wire off, but I hate it. General Sheffield is counting on us. He's got everything he owns tied up in this line. I guess we owe him the best we can give. Come over to the coach and let's have a drink." At that moment Tom Love slowly walked by and the colonel grabbed his shirtsleeve. "Tom, you're an old hand. Come on and have a drink with us. I got a couple of things to talk over."

When they reached the colonel's quarters, Weatherall and Love found chairs while the colonel scrounged three glasses and poured the bourbon. The colonel hefted his drink, said, "To better times," and downed his whiskey. After refilling his glass, he sank into a chair. "Tomorrow we start making track."

"Sounds good to me," Tom said. He took his corncob from his pocket and thumbed tobacco into the bowl. Tom's demeanor, usually good-natured, was serious, and for once he wasn't smiling. "How do we get the supplies to Canon City?"

"We don't," the colonel said, and explained Weatherall's plan.

Tom passed a match over his pipe's bowl. "Smart thinking. You might expect Creed to come up with an idea like that."

Weatherall swallowed a finger of bourbon. He wanted to go home, take a bath, and sleep for a week, but the colonel wanted to talk. He was under a lot of pressure and needed this outlet. Weatherall noticed how old the colonel looked suddenly. Big brown bags sagged like half-moons under both eyes, while deep furrows lined his cheeks and forehead. When a man accepted responsibility, he paid a price.

The colonel dipped his cigar butt into the bourbon. "I dread what lies ahead. I knew the moment Adams hired Dallas Mason things would get worse. We're going to have trouble every mile of the way."

"We've been having trouble," Creed said. "But not bad trouble. We're beyond dirty tricks now. They aren't paying a gunman to yank up railroad ties."

Weatherall's tongue pushed out three wobbly smoke rings. "I don't think Dallas wants trouble any more than we do. He had us in a bag yesterday, and he let us out."

"That's a fact," Tom said, and nodded, his constant optimism surfacing. "He could have killed us, burned the wagons, shot the mules. He seemed to go out of his way to avoid trouble."

The colonel clamped down on the bourbon-soaked cigar, sprinkling ashes that whitened his beard. "I don't care what he did yesterday. It doesn't change the facts. Adams means to beat us to Leadville, and it's Mason's job to see that he does. There's too much money involved here. Sooner or later someone is going to get killed."

"I think you're too hard on Dallas," Weatherall said. "I've known him a long time. He'll try to stop us with brains, not bullets."

"You sound very certain."

"I am. Dallas is no Jesse James or William Quantrill. Dallas won't use a gun unless he's forced to."

Tom drank the last of his whiskey and glanced over at the colonel expectantly. "I have to agree with Creed. After all, he and Dallas are old friends."

Weatherall pushed his Stetson back on his head, breathed a weary sigh. He was glad Tom had backed him, though he wasn't surprised. Tom was always supportive, positive. Weatherall had never met a man, besides Tom, who was held in high regard by all who knew him. Even Tully Williams liked Tom. When a man like Tom backed you, it meant something.

The colonel poured more whiskey into Tom's empty glass. Glancing at Creed, who shook his head, he popped the cork back into the bottle. Tom puffed contentedly on his corncob while Weatherall considered the inchlong ash on his cigar. A cool breeze ruffled the curtain, and the stale odor of tobacco mingled with the warm smell of bourbon.

The colonel pulled his fingers across his chin, gaze steadying on Weatherall. "Dallas didn't have just railroad men when he stopped you, did he?"

"No, he didn't."

"You said he had sixteen men in all. How many do you think were hard cases?"

"Five. Six."

"It always comes down to this. All right. Adams is hiring gunhands; then we're going to hire some too."

"I don't think that's the way, Colonel."

"Holy cow! What other way is there? You have to fight fire with fire."

"So far there haven't been any fights."

"There will be. Tom, what do you think?"

Tom rubbed the tips of his fingers together. "I'm inclined to see this your way, Colonel. Most railroad men wear a gun only because they have to. Except for a few toughs, most of 'em aren't looking for trouble and couldn't stand up to Dallas and his kind. But Creed knows his business. He must have some reason for going against hiring guns."

"Then spell it out, Creed."

Weatherall downed his bourbon, leaned forward, and rested both elbows on the table. "When you hire that kind of people, you advertise that you're looking for trouble. Tension's bound to increase in both camps. Plus, there's one more thing. Those men live by a different set of rules than the rest of us. They're hard to control. Not only that, but if we start bringing in toughs, the Colorado will just bring in more. You've said yourself this is the roughest hell-on-wheels camp you've ever been in. You haven't seen anything until you load this place with hired killers."

"But you want Jess to hire some guns to hold the Royal Gorge."

"That's different. The gorge is our lifeline. If we have to fight there, then we fight."

"What about here?"

"Leave things the way they are. We can handle it. They tear up track; we tear up track. They burn ties; we burn ties. But no shooting."

"What do you think, Tom?"

"Colonel, this ain't my line of work, but it is Creed's. I'm for whatever he says."

"All right. We play it Creed's way." The colonel gulped down his bourbon. "I appreciate your time. I know you're both worn out and want to get some rest. We'll talk again."

Nelly May Scott sat before her dresser, pulling a comb through her long blond tresses. The day's heat had faded, but she wore a loose shift, not wanting to wrinkle the ankle-length black gown that would be her uniform tonight. This was her best time of day and her worst. The long, lonely afternoon lay behind her. She would be with people, so some of the loneliness would pass. But only some, because in Bullard's tented Emporium, she knew a different kind of loneliness, the loneliness of knowing that things would never change. That no good man would ever care for a woman like her. That only the same emptiness lay ahead.

136

Not that she felt sorry for herself, or that she would want to return to the life she'd led before, even if she could. She never looked back, never regretted leaving the farm. That life of abuse and drudgery had been worse than this one. Her life was her own, whereas before it had belonged to others. Still, she understood that she had long ago cut herself off from what everyone needed: friends, respect, love.

She was an outsider, but she had made herself one. Looking back over her twenty-two years, she could see that she had willfully made every decision that had brought her where she was. At times, such as now, she hated this life because it was so superficial. However, the job itself didn't touch her. She had learned to separate her mind from her body at age twelve, when, a year after her mother's death, her father had forced her into his bedroom. That experience had terrified her, scarred her. To live with the years that followed, she had taught herself to blot out the heaving, sweating body above her. Now, ten years later, when she brought someone to her tent, she was untouched by what followed. She could do it while eating an apple or reading a magazine, if she knew how to read. Because what happened held no meaning for her, she was dumbfounded at the importance men

137

attached to the activity. It always amazed her that a man would hand over a day's hard-earned pay for five minutes of rutting and grunting.

Certainly, as a young girl she'd had ideas of love. During the long days when she'd cooked, cleaned, washed clothes, and served as a mother for her six younger brothers and sisters, she'd dreamed that someone would ride up and carry her away to a world of excitement and romance. So on that morning when Brett Swinford, a drummer, had stopped to water his horse, his stories fell on waiting ears. At fifteen, she'd already possessed a woman's beauty, and Brett had read her like a catalogue. In less than two hours, he'd convinced her to throw off her slave's apron and accompany him to what he promised was a world of dreams. But Brett had never delivered. She'd spent a great deal of the six months they were together on her back, making money to pay Brett's bills. He'd called it love, and because he'd been tender and kind, not brutal and demanding like her father, she'd been stupid enough to believe it.

When Brett had tired of her, she'd found work at a saloon because the only other jobs she was prepared for were housework and cooking. Not that she'd wanted to work as a prostitute, but it was that or sling hash. She'd had her fill of that kind of life before she had run off with Brett.

She had a penchant for attracting the wrong kind of man. After Brett, she'd met George Ives, a gambler, who'd convinced her that he couldn't live without her. Like an idiot, she'd followed George around for two years. George hadn't set her up in a room, but he'd been a difficult man to live with, a difficult man to please. At times, he had become violent. Her kidneys still ached as a mute reminder of his temper. Then one day, she'd found herself alone, stuck with a hotel bill she could pay off only one way.

George had soured her on men, destroyed all her girlish fancies. After him, she trusted no man. She used them as they used her. In her mind, men were nothing but animals. She took care of their needs for a price. A high price.

And then, a few months back, Jim Smith had entered her world. He seemed self-conscious, naive, sensitive, but she'd pegged his easy, outgoing way as an act. He was just a man, only smarter than most. His boyish enthusiasm almost made a woman want to mother him, but she knew that, underneath, he was like all the rest.

Still, as time passed, she had begun to

wonder about him. When he came to Bullard's, he always sought her out, was quick to buy drinks or dance tickets, but not once had he suggested retiring to her tent. She hadn't been able to figure him out; it bothered her. What did he want? Why did he invest his time and money in drinks and dances, yet never in the one thing that men seemed to feel was of overwhelming importance?

Grudgingly, she'd come to trust Jim. She enjoyed his company and looked forward to the time she spent with him almost every evening. However, in the past few weeks that liking had turned to something stronger, so she'd tried to avoid him. That had been impossible. Her job was to be nice to Bullard's guests, so she'd been forced to talk with Jim, drink with Jim, dance with Jim. Being with him had become a terrible strain. His unpolished ways, his quick smile, which once had put her at ease, now left her flustered.

She laid her brush on the dresser and stared at her reflection in the mirror. She was in love with Jim, and that made her a complete fool. Still, she couldn't ignore her feelings. He was the only man who had ever treated her as a person, not a thing. Even though he knew exactly what she was. Every night she left the Emporium with a man trailing behind. And more than one man. She made her money pleasing men, not pushing dance tickets and drinks.

Jim was honest. Decent. He had values. There could never be a place in his life for a woman such as she. He liked her, she didn't doubt that. Still, Jim had plans. He needed a wife he could be proud of. They could be friends, but they could never be anything more.

Which brought her to Tully Williams. Tully acted as if he owned her; and he harbored a deep resentment toward Jim. This was another reason she tried to avoid Jim. If he continued spending time with her, it meant trouble. Tully was a mean-spirited individual who liked to push people around. He threatened Jim often, but since Jim wouldn't back off, Tully would one day do more than threaten. His pride demanded it. She didn't want to cause trouble between them, because Tully could beat Jim senseless. It made her stomach turn over to think of it.

Everything came back to the heart of the problem. Why did Jim bother? Why his interest? He was almost brotherly in his efforts to persuade her to find another profession.

An hour later she headed for Bullard's Emporium. Lil Kiner and Laura Holden walked

141

just ahead of her, but she lagged behind deliberately. She would have more than enough company before this night was over; besides, what could they talk about? She preferred the cool evening air, the vast descending darkness with its scattered points of starlight.

Once in the Emporium, Nelly May stood at the bar and surveyed the huge tent. In the left-hand corner, beyond the boot-scuffed dance floor, the dance band tuned its instruments. At the front of the room sat chairs and tables, and to the right, the crap table. As Nelly May faced the fifty-foot glass mirror beyond the bar, she saw Tom Love's hefty form appear in the polished glass as he strolled through the open tent flap.

Tom spotted her and steered over to the mahogany. "You sure look nice. Black must be your color."

"You're in early tonight. Amos, why don't you give our first customer a drink on the house?"

Bullard swung around from where he had been checking stock, his bland saloon-owner's face showing a forced smile. "Good idea. Max, pour the man a drink."

When the barkeep poured two ounces, Nelly May repressed a chuckle. She knew how tight Bullard was. This free drink would give him ulcers. "How's the work going, Tom?"

"Made five miles today. So did the Colorado."

Nelly May crossed both arms over her breasts, turned, and leaned back against the bar. She always felt comfortable with Tom. He claimed to have a wife back in Frisco. If so, he remained true to her. Nelly May had never seen Tom go out back with a woman. Not that he was perfect — he drank too much, and he was a heavy gambler. But he was one of the few men she'd ever liked.

"What brings you in so early?" she asked.

"I wanted to talk to you."

Instantly, her body grew rigid. She knew what he wanted to talk about. She said, "Let's find a table," and led him to a spot removed from the bar. "You know there's nothing I can do."

"You can avoid him."

"Tom, I don't seek Jim out. It's the other way around."

"Then insult him."

"Amos wouldn't like that. I have to work here."

"Then step on him. Hurt his feelings. Do something to drive him away."

"I can't do that."

"You know Tully is going to beat the hell out of him one of these days."

"Good God! You know I'd do anything I

could to stop that."

"There's one thing you can do. Go back to Denver."

"Tom, I'm making too much money."

"Does money mean that much to you?"

"Tom, I won't look this way forever. I've got to make it while I can. I've got to think of myself."

"Doesn't Jim mean anything to you?"

Her red mouth squared defiantly as her breath caught in her throat. "This is a hard world. A woman has to look out for herself. No one forces Jim to come here. He's no fool. He knows how Tully feels."

Tom's left hand lifted his corncob from his vest pocket. As he tamped tobacco into the pipe, his jawline firmed. "I've always thought of you as a fine woman, despite what you do. I guess I was wrong."

"I'm no angel. I never pretended to be. I'm on my own, Tom. I have to look out for myself."

Holding the unlit pipe in his fist, Tom got to his feet. "At least I tried. When Jim ends up in the company hospital, you just remember who put him there."

As Tom's footsteps faded toward the tent flap, she laid her head in her hands and closed her eyes. Damn Tom for blaming all this on her! She didn't know what to do. She didn't want to see Jim hurt, but she couldn't talk to Tully. That would only make him more aggressive. For some reason, he didn't like Jim, and she sensed that Tully's dislike went beyond Jim's interest in her. Despite Tom's suggestion, she couldn't leave camp. She had to think of the future. When she was forty, and ugly, and broke, Jim wouldn't be there to pick her up. It was a hard world. Jim had to look out for himself.

Two hours later, Nelly May sat at a table sharing a drink with a bearded tie-setter from the Colorado line. The man was lonely. All he'd done for the past sixty minutes was talk about his wife and children. Not that she minded listening. She understood loneliness, and his devotion to his family intrigued her. Most men in camp, married or not, were interested in two items: gambling and sex. Now the Colorado man seemed to be running out of talk, so he just puffed on his pipe and stared at his whiskey glass.

She glanced around the tent. She didn't see an empty space at the bar, and the tables were surrounded by railroaders chatting with Bullard's hostesses or playing cards. She spotted Dallas Mason talking with Amos Bullard, who stood with his head tipped back so that he could look Dallas in the face. Dallas was here almost every night. He loved poker and also spent a lot of time out back. She was glad that Dallas had never approached her. She knew why he was in camp, and Creed Weatherall had always been decent to her, which was more than she could say for most men.

As the band swung into the opening notes of "Over the Waves," her bearded companion pushed to his feet. "I guess I'd best get back to camp. Talk to you again sometime." He swung toward the open flap and her gaze, following, settled on Jim Smith, who was just coming in. His boyish features brightened with recognition as he hustled up to the table. "Didn't think I'd be lucky enough to find you alone."

Her shoulders shrugged in a resigned gesture when he took the chair opposite her. At the same time, her heart hit an unsteady beat. She didn't want him here, yet his being here was everything. She remembered what Tom had said, and her breasts rose and fell with her deep breaths. She didn't want Jim hurt. Certainly not because of her.

Jim signaled the waiter for drinks and fired up a cigar. "Place is busy tonight."

"Every night." She watched him try to blow a smoke ring. He had been trying to blow smoke rings as long as she'd known him, but he wouldn't give up.

The waiter set two drinks on the table, and Jim dropped seventy-five cents on the tray. As the waiter rounded to another table, Jim lifted his glass. "Here's to the prettiest girl in camp."

Nelly May didn't bother with her drink. "Why do you spend your time with me? Why don't you spend it with Lil? You love to dance, and she's the best dancer in the place."

"I love talking to you."

"Why? We always plow the same ground. It's not getting us anywhere. Maybe Lil could take you out back and show you what life's all about."

The hurt in his eyes moved her. She wanted to touch his cheek. To take his hand. To say she didn't mean it. But she had to do something before Tully half-killed him.

"I'm surprised you'd say a thing like that."

"You're wasting your time with me. There's no sense in it."

"I enjoy your company."

"Why?"

"I feel comfortable with you. Look, I'm no woman's man. It's not easy for me to talk with a girl. But I don't have any trouble with you."

"You need practice. You could have a lot of fun with Lil."

"If I wanted to go out back with someone,

I wouldn't ask Lil."

Her eyes challenged him. "Who would you ask?"

"Never mind."

"And if I asked you?"

"I wouldn't go."

Her gaze dropped to the table, but she kept her professional smile. His words cut because they reinforced the distance between them. It was his nature to help people, and so he took the time to try to point her in another direction. But his kindness was all she would ever know. When she looked in a mirror, she understood that what she was, was the one thing most men wanted. But it wasn't enough for Jim.

She looked out on the dance floor, where painted women, dressed in brightly colored gowns that revealed their shoulders and upper breasts, struggled to keep time with drunken men. The tent smelled of sweat, tobacco smoke, and cheap whiskey, and it made her feel sick. This was no place for anyone. There was no life here. Only the illusion of life.

A puff of smoke escaped Jim's lips. "Nelly May, why don't you go back to Denver?"

"I've told you I have no talent. What could I do there that I can't do here?"

"So you don't sing well enough to get on-stage. There are other ways to make a living.

You like to sew. You make most of your own clothes. Maybe you could open a millinery shop."

"And make twenty-five or thirty dollars a month."

"This is no place for you. Why can't you see that?"

"Why don't you stop acting like I'm your younger sister? I am what I am. Why can't you accept it?"

"Can't you understand that this is a dangerous way to live?"

"You're the one who can't seem to understand that."

Jim shook his head and sighed. "Why argue? Let's get some tickets and dance."

As Nelly May rose to her feet, she saw Tully striding purposefully forward. He reached the table, his acne-pitted cheeks aflame. "I told you to stay away from him."

"Jim's a customer. It's my job to drink with the customers."

"Then drink with somebody else." Tully's fingers pressed into her upper arm. "Come on. You're wasting time with this chump."

Jim surged out of his chair. His lips pulled wide in an odd grimace, while his sun-bronzed complexion turned a shade whiter. "Nelly May and I were just about to have a dance."

Tully put one big hand on Jim's chest and

shoved him back into his chair. "Forget the dance, and don't get out of that chair unless you want your face rearranged."

Nelly May's breath caught in her throat. She saw Tully hover over Jim, and she could smell the hate beating out of the big man. Jim's boyish features seemed slack and undefined. He licked his lips, glanced uncertainly at Nelly May. The tent had quietened. Men at nearby tables sat with their heads lowered, looking at their cards or their drinks. These men liked Jim. They knew he didn't stand a chance against Tully. But they couldn't interfere. No matter what they might think, they would remain neutral. Custom dictated it.

One quick step put her between the two men. Her hand caught Tully's shoulders. "Don't be a fool. Amos won't allow any trouble in here. It's bad for business."

A shuddering breath tore between Tully's clenched teeth. His eyes, wild and angry, reached beyond her to hit Jim like the impact of a fist. "Stay away from her, or I'll catch you in the streets some night and put the boots to you."

Out of nowhere, Amos Bullard appeared, flanked by four muscular bouncers. "Any problem here?"

Indigestion burned Nelly May's chest, but

she managed a smile. "No problem. Tully and I were just going to the bar."

When they swung away from the table, she saw Bullard nod to Jim and say in a low voice, "Just say the word, and I'll put an end to your problem with that bum."

"I can take care of my own trouble."

"I'm not so sure," Bullard replied before he motioned his men to their posts and ambled toward the craps table.

Nelly May felt Tully's arm encircle her waist as he urged her toward the bar. She knew Jim was watching, and regret flooded her. But although Jim was hurt, perhaps it was for the best. He must realize what she was, accept it, and get out of her life. He wasn't her kind of man. Tully was. When it came to the opposite sex, Tully was the story of her life.

When Tully ordered the drinks, she sneaked a glance over her shoulder. Jim's features looked dried-up and defenseless. Suddenly, she realized that Jim was afraid. Deathly afraid. She also realized that Jim wouldn't back off from seeing her. It didn't make sense.

Tully jerked her against him. He caught her jaw between his thumb and forefinger and lifted her face to his. "I don't want you to spend any more time with that shrimp. Got it?"

"Tully, I work here. I'm paid to entertain the customers."

"Find somebody else."

"Why do you get so upset about Jim? All we ever do is talk."

"That's all he's capable of. He doesn't know the meaning of the word 'man.' I hate his guts."

"Why? What did Jim ever do to you?"

"I've known this kind before. He never has to work for anything. Everything just comes his way. It's always the opposite with me. I never had any luck. I've had to work like a dog to make it."

"That's not Jim's fault."

"The hell it isn't. His kind are always playing up to the boss. They're nothing but a bunch of apple polishers. I'd love a chance to push his face in."

Tully nuzzled her hair and trailed a finger across her bare shoulder. Absentmindedly, she picked up the glass the barkeep set before her. Things were worse than she'd imagined. She'd thought Tully was jealous, but it was clear now that she was no more than a pawn in his twisted scheme to hurt Jim. If he couldn't use her, he'd find something else. There was no way she could prevent what Jim faced. She looked up at Tully. He was an arrogant, bitter, unlikable man. When his hand moved down her back to settle possessively on her buttock, her throat tightened.

"Finish your drink and let's get out of here," he said.

She nodded and tossed the drink down. As they turned from the bar, she saw Jim's unhappy face reflected in the mirror. As Tully led her out the back, for the second time in her life she understood shame.

CHAPTER 8

At ten o'clock Sunday morning, Weatherall stood near the corral, looking west. He'd arrived from Canon City about noon yesterday, and it felt good to have a day off and relax with a smooth cigar. Last night after supper, he and Charlotte and Will Johnson had played fan tan until eleven o'clock. They'd spent a pleasant evening, caught up in cards and small talk, the railroad forgotten for a few short hours. They'd been making track toward Canon City now for two weeks and had covered sixty miles. Soon they would bridge the Arkansas River. He looked south, at the Colorado camp. They'd been making track too, matching the Denver rails mile for mile.

Weatherall exhaled a smoke ring, his gray eyes dark with thought. There had been no hint of trouble since Dallas had stopped the supply train, but this peaceful coexistence couldn't last. He knew that a Colorado freight train was over in Canon City, waiting for a chance to invade the Royal Gorge and start blasting grade. However, Jess Strawberry had forted up the gorge, and, as of yet, no attempt had been made to breech the logged-off entrance. Still, both lines were only about sixty miles from Canon City, so something had to break, and soon. Weatherall hated the thought of trouble — but at least, when it arrived, he could stop worrying and face it.

Footsteps scuffed behind Weatherall, and he heeled around to find a serious-faced Jim Smith approaching. Weatherall blew out a thin stream of smoke as Jim halted beside him. "You look like a man with something on his mind."

Jim fiddled with his fingers. He didn't look at Weatherall, but instead hooked a boot over the corral's lowest rung and, propping his forearms on the top rung, stared out across the distance.

Weatherall leaned against a fence post, studying the youngster. "Looks like you lost a little weight."

"A little."

A mule nickered from the stable. The land's earthy smell rode the breeze. Weatherall's back itched, so he scrubbed it back and forth across the fence post. Jim's attitude bothered him. Jim was always friendly, animated, cheerful. But this morning he seemed subdued.

Jim pushed erect, but he kept his gaze on

the ground. "Creed, I need some advice."

"I can give you some, but I don't think you'll like it."

"What do you mean?"

"Stay away from Bullard's, and stay away from Nelly May."

"I have to pass the time somewhere."

"Then pass it somewhere else. Nelly May's nothing but trouble."

Jim swung around to face Weatherall. "I think I'm in love with her."

"You're not in love with her. She's good-looking and has more class than most of her kind, so you want to change her life. Forget it. You don't change women like Nelly May."

"I thought you were the one person who would understand. After all, Charlotte was a saloon woman when you met her."

"Charlotte was a dealer. She didn't make her living drinking colored water and lying on her back."

Jim turned the color of warm ashes as his Adam's apple bobbed up and down. "I'm sorry I bothered you."

Weatherall reached out to pull Jim around as the youngster spun away. "Look, I like Nelly May. She's straight. But you've got to face up to what she is. What she does."

"I know what she does."

"Do you really believe you can forget all

the men she's been with?"

"I can try."

"That may not be enough. But let's say it is. What are you going to do when you run into someone from the old days?"

Jim's lips tightened as a helpless expression pocked his face. "Creed, I don't know what to do. I've stayed away from Bullard's for two weeks. I'm a nervous wreck. She's all I think about."

"We haven't mentioned the most important thing. How does the lady feel about you?"

"I don't know."

"Wouldn't it be better to find out before you drive yourself crazy?"

"You know Nelly May. You can't touch her. Inside, I mean."

"She's like all saloon women. They close up. Have to. Otherwise they'd get hurt. That's a hard life."

"Do you think I ought to talk to her?"

"If that's the only way you can get her out of your system."

"Maybe I'll ask her to go away with me."

"She wouldn't do that no matter how she feels. It wouldn't work. People wouldn't let it work."

"I've heard of cases where it worked."

"That's the exception, not the rule. But,

like I said, you won't listen to me. You don't want advice. You want me to say it's all right. Well, it's all right. It's your life. Live it."

Jim bit into his lower lip. His blond head dipped, and he stared at the ground.

Weatherall puffed on his cigar. He'd been afraid something like this would happen. Jim was young. Good-hearted. Inexperienced. Nelly May Scott was a beautiful woman, and it was her job to make men like her. Weatherall gazed off to one side. Grunted. Nelly May was a decent sort. Maybe he should talk to her, ask her to let Jim down easy. Still, this was none of his business. Jim would have to handle it as best he could.

Jim cleared his throat. "There's one more problem."

"Tully?"

"Creed, I'm afraid of him."

"You ought to be. He's a mean one."

"Am I a coward?"

"Not from what I've seen."

"Then why don't I call Tully's bluff?"

"It's no bluff. Look, nobody wants to get busted up."

"I've never been in a fight in my life. I don't know what to do."

"This is a railroad camp. I could talk to Tully."

"Amos made that offer twice, and he meant more than talk."

"Why don't you take Amos up on it?"

"I just can't. It's odd. I'm scared to death, but for some reason I can't walk away from this."

"I know what you mean. I've been there. Pride's a thing that can cause a man lots of grief."

"I guess the best thing is to call Tully out and get it over with."

"Maybe, but not yet. You've got to get a better hold on yourself. You need some sleep, and you'd better start eating again. A few more days won't matter. Besides, you and me got our work cut out."

"You're going to teach me how to fight?"

"I'm gonna try."

Jim's hands made a popping sound. "Boy, I remember when you tore into Roy Stone at Reno."

"You might also remember he licked me."

"Mick Wilson didn't."

"After supper, meet me out behind the barn. And let's keep this quiet."

Jim grabbed Weatherall's hand. "Thanks, Creed. I feel better already."

As the youngster swung back toward main camp, Weatherall stuck his cigar between his teeth. He didn't like what lay ahead. Jim was in for a beating. A little sparring, some advice on how to hit and where to hit, might build up Jim's confidence, but it wouldn't change the outcome. Weatherall stared south toward the river. He felt sorry for Jim, but in a man's world, there were some things you couldn't run from.

The clang of tin cups hitting tabletops, and metal forks scraping tin plates lifted from the mess hall up to the corner table occupied by Weatherall, Charlotte, the colonel, and Will Johnson. The tent flaps were rolled down to keep out the morning chill, as the sun had not yet peaked to burn off the five-thirty mist. The thick odor of black coffee laced the tent, and the smell of eggs and sausage fried in heavy grease washed out from the kitchen.

Al, the mess attendant, filled four cups with steaming coffee, then hurried back to the kitchen to fetch their breakfasts. Weatherall rubbed his eyes then shook his head. "I will never get used to waking up at five o'clock. Even the birds are sleeping."

Charlotte patted his thigh. "That marshal's job spoiled you. Now you have to work for a living."

The colonel slurped his coffee. "Whew! That's hot. You know, I never could understand how a man could lie around in bed until noon. This is the best time of day. Cool. Quiet. Gives a person a chance to pull things together. Right, Will?"

The rolling-stock boss grunted. He was never one to say much, and until he'd eaten breakfast, he said nothing.

Waiting for his coffee to cool, Weatherall took out his timepiece, wound the stem, and replaced the watch in his vest pocket. It beat all how these people could be so full of life. He'd be in a fog for another hour. His head turned toward Charlotte, and she gave him a ready smile. Even at this ungodly hour, she was absolutely beautiful.

Al laid their platters before them, checked the coffepot, and returned to the kitchen. The colonel sliced off a chunk of sausage, forked it into his mouth. His brown eyes gleamed with pleasure as he chewed. Will sipped his coffee, dug into the scrambled eggs. Charlotte buttered her bread, then passed the loaf to Weatherall, who set it disinterestedly on the table. How could anyone be hungry? It wasn't even daylight.

Horse hooves raced toward the mess hall. A voice shouted. "Whoa! Whoa!" and a gray-faced track hand raced into the tent, long legs pumping him up to the colonel's table. "Colonel, we got hit about midnight. They blew up a bunch of track. It's a hell of a mess

161

out there." He spotted Charlotte and swept off his hat. "Excuse the language, Missus Weatherall."

The colonel swallowed his sausage. His mouth gulped for words. "Holy cow! Anybody hurt?"

"No."

"Thank God for that. Now what happened?"

"A bunch led by Dallas Mason rode in about midnight. There wasn't anything we could do. They started planting dynamite. It was as simple as that."

The colonel surged to his feet. "We'd better get out there."

"Colonel, it's done. You might as well finish your breakfast. Nothing's going to change. We'll look it over later," Weatherall said.

A groan escaped the colonel's lips. He nodded. "I guess you're right. We may be in for a long day. Might as well get started on a full stomach."

After the track hand turned back to the mess hall, Weatherall forced his fork into the eggs. Dallas had played it smart. He'd waited until they'd reached the point where they had to bridge the river. Without track, they'd find that an impossible task. The eggs tasted like a mouthful of mush, so Weatherall sprinkled more salt and pepper on them. He had to accept the blame for what had happened. Trouble was his responsibility. That was twice Dallas had gotten the jump on him.

Talk surged up from the main mess hall as men discussed the news. Weatherall felt Charlotte's gaze on him, but he didn't look at her. She understood what he was thinking. She'd say something like "It's not your fault," but he knew better. He pushed his plate away, leaned back, crossed his arms over his chest. Glancing to his right, he saw the animated faces of the people he worked with, engaged in muted conversation, but talk at his table had ceased.

Early sun brightened the tent flaps. Outside a dog barked to the west. The colonel shoved back from the table. "All right, men. Let's move out."

"Colonel, can I ride out and see how things are?" Charlotte asked.

"Why not? Do the men good to have a beautiful woman to look at."

"You always know what to say. If you were twenty years younger, I'd leave Creed for you."

"If I were twenty years younger, I'd take you away from him."

"That would be a full-time job," Weatherall said, and as the tension eased a bit, they all laughed.

Metal wheels screeched against metal rails as the train shuddered to a halt. Weatherall jumped down from the first car and, turning, lifted his arms to help Charlotte to the ground while the rest of the crew dismounted. They rushed to the front of the hissing engine, where an angry "Holy cow!" burst from the colonel's lips. Twisted rails lay scattered over the prairie. Broken and splintered ties covered the ground, and huge holes had been blasted in the earth where the dynamite had been set. The stock of extra rails and ties had been thrown into the river; some ties could be seen, half-submerged.

Will Johnson spat out a fleck of tobacco juice. "This is going to put us at least a week behind."

The colonel scratched his beard, cursed under his breath. "They did a thorough job." He turned to Lee Keene and George Duncan, who had been part of the holding team here at the end of the tracks. "How many miles out are we?"

"I'd say six or seven," Keene said.

The colonel pulled at his beard. "Will, get the men to cleaning this mess up. I'm headed back to main camp. We'll move everything up here. This is going to be a twenty-four-hour-a-day job."

A seven-thirty sun burned off the morning dew. A wren whistled from a clump of stunted piñon. Weatherall turned toward the river, his gaze following the Colorado's westward-moving rails. In the distance, he could see tiny figures silhouetted against the skyline. The Colorado was making track.

The colonel clumped up to him. "I'm going to get a work train out here by dark. We'll send a flatcar with new tools and a forge, three 'sowbellies,' a dining car, a cooking car, and two supply cars. Then we can move everything out. We're too far from the end of the line."

Smoke swirled up from Weatherall's cigar as he shook out his match. "I'm against it. We've lost some track and some time but nobody's dead. Anyway, they could blow up the track behind us."

The colonel squeezed his forehead. He looked worried. "I guess you're right. We can't set up guards from here to Denver." He shoved his hand deep into his pockets and glared toward the Colorado's distant work crew. "Holy cow! Just once I'd like to build a railroad. That's trouble enough without all this other nonsense thrown in."

Iron clanged against iron. Men grunted as they tossed broken ties into a heap. Heat radiated from the locomotive, and the damp odor of steam lifted from the engine box. "What are we going to do?" the colonel asked.

A smoke ring broke from Weatherall's lips. "Give 'em a dose of their own medicine."

Charlotte's hand closed over Weatherall's left arm. "Won't they be expecting that?"

"They'll be expecting it."

"We need to send to Pueblo for some gunhands," the colonel said.

"You know how I feel about that."

"But, Creed, these men are railroaders. They can't stand up to Dallas and his toughs."

"I think they can."

Charlotte's fingers tightened on Weatherall's arm. Her green eyes darkened. "Someone could get killed."

"Not likely." Weatherall gave her hand a reassuring pat. She was right, of course, but he wasn't about to let her know it.

Twilight shaded the loamy plains. Downwind an owl hooted. As the ten men waded into the river, the eastward-flowing current threatened to take with it the wooden raft they had constructed to protect their boots, guns, and ammunition. The bottom mud squished under their bare feet as the river gurgled around them. Upon reaching the south side, they lifted the raft from the water

166

and climbed onto dry land.

The twilight had faded to a darkness that made blurred shapes out of solid figures. Weatherall pulled on his boots, stood up, and strapped on his gunbelt. In the distance, a yellow glow marked the fire at the Colorado's end of the track. After the other men had their boots on and had gotten to their feet, Weatherall handed out shotguns. "Remember, we don't want a fight if we can avoid it."

Someone behind Weatherall sucked in a deep breath. A second man cleared his throat. The crew was nervous and Weatherall couldn't blame them. They were workingmen who had probably never pointed a gun at anyone in their lives. But he felt confident they'd hold their own. "One last thing. Hopefully, there won't be any problem, but if you have to shoot, shoot to kill. That's a tough bunch up there."

He moved ahead, with the others following. This was soft, level land, and it was easy to advance noiselessly. He knew his remark about killing had made this group a bit queasy, but it was better to face facts. He hoped it wouldn't come to killing. Killing changed a man. It left an emptiness that never completely went away.

Almost before he knew it, the Colorado

wagons appeared, solid shapes in the dark, and he motioned his crew to hit the dirt. Four men sat around a fire drinking coffee, and he saw Dallas Mason sitting nearby carving a piece of wood. A sixth individual puffed on a pipe. A band of horses grazed to the south. Weatherall held his position. He wanted to be certain that all hands were accounted for, and one or two men might be in the wagon. Tension knotted his chest, and he knew that same tension unsettled his companions. They had to be filled with doubt, worry, fear. But they held their positions.

Phosphorus flowered in a small, yellow explosion as the fellow near the rails brought a match to his pipe. When one of the horses off to the left snorted, Weatherall's breath stopped. They were upwind from those horses. Any sudden movement on their part would panic the animals. Weatherall muttered a soft "Damn!" No matter how well one planned things, something unexpected always happened. One of the men by the fire pulled a pack of cards from his saddlebags and dealt out four hands. Dallas concentrated on his carving.

Weatherall waved his left hand, and five men headed off in that direction. He waved his right hand, and the rest of the group crawled to their positions. He wanted to form a semicircle to the south, with the river forming a natural barrier to the north. When his bunch was spaced out, he waved them ahead, and they made their way slowly toward the Colorado outfit. Weatherall planned to work in close enough so that the shotguns would prevent any thought of gunplay. His people probably couldn't hit a boxcar with a pistol, but with a shotgun all one did was point it and squeeze the trigger. That fact wouldn't be lost on Dallas.

Despite the cool breeze on his damp shirt, sweat bathed Weatherall's body. They needed to cover about fifty yards before they could get the drop on Dallas's outfit. The breeze strengthened, and one of the horses snorted again while two others lifted their heads nervously. The guard caught that tension. He stood erect as his gaze swept the flat countryside. The cardplayers dropped their cards, and Dallas glanced up from his whittling. He walked out to where the fire's glow ended, his angular face alert and cautious. Weatherall and his men flattened against the ground and waited as hollow pits sucked at their bellies.

After what seemed like ten years, the horses resumed their grazing. Dallas strolled back toward the fire, where he resumed his carving. The four cardplayers picked up their hands. The horses had quieted, but their heads still dipped up and down while soft nickers marked their uneasiness.

Weatherall motioned with one hand, and his men inched forward. Dallas's crew had relaxed, and it was too dark to spot the figures approaching at ground level. If only the horses didn't spook again, a few more minutes would close the distance. Now he could smell the smoke from the juniper-stoked fire that formed dancing dots before his smoke-streaked eyes.

As Weatherall and his crew climbed to their feet, Dallas caught sight of the motion. He grabbed his revolver and shouted, "Look out! We got company."

Weatherall's calm voice cut the night. "You're staring down the barrels of nine shotguns, Dallas. Don't be a fool."

A resigned expression loosened Dallas's features. He shoved his gun in his holster. "Ease off, boys. This round belongs to them."

Revolvers hit the ground while the Colorado outfit waited in strained silence. Weatherall's group edged into the firelight's flickering circle. "Dallas, you and your men drop your gunbelts and move over by the far wagon."

After the order was carried out, Weatherall holstered his six-shooter and lit a cigar. He released a stream of white smoke and felt some of his tension ride out with it. They'd been lucky. It wasn't often that things worked out so well. He exhaled smoke, let it trickle through his nostrils. For some reason, he was hungry. Thirst, he could have understood. But hunger? "Jim, pick up those guns and toss them in the river."

Dallas took a forward step. "Creed, that forty-four means a lot to me. I bought it the day I was appointed a United States deputy marshal. I won't cause any trouble. You have my word."

"Fine. Go over and pick it up. Jim, dump the rest in the river."

A shaky crewman stared incredulously at Weatherall and said, "You're going to put a gun in his hand?"

"His word's good with me."

Bloom grimaced. "I'd rather kiss a rattle-snake."

Wind ruffled the wagon tops as Dallas swung around Creed and strolled over to pick up his gunbelt. While he buckled it around his waist, Jim gathered up the other sidearms and carried them to the river. Ace Benson threw another log on the fire, and the Denver men fidgeted uncertainly. Weatherall took another relaxing pull on his cigar. He studied the faces of the Colorado crew fronting them. They were noncommittal. These men were professionals. They would play the game as it unfolded. He hated to leave his people with this bunch. One careless moment would put those shotguns in different hands.

He took four steps forward and with his boot heel dug a line fronting the wagon. "Ace, I want you and Ted and E.J. to keep your guns on these boys. If they cross the line, shoot 'em. I didn't say, Think about it. I said, Shoot. They'll overrun you if you give them half a chance. Tom, get some help. Jim, you and Steve burn the ties. Then dump all the tools in the river. Lee, you and George set the dynamite."

After the men sprang into action, Weatherall turned and strolled to the fire, where Dallas stood with his thumbs hooked in his belt. "Well, Creed, you're doing a thorough job of it."

"That's the idea."

"I knew you'd hit us, but I wasn't expecting you so soon."

"That's what I hoped for. I didn't want any shooting."

"It's best this way. We'll just bring some new stuff out tomorrow."

"Yeah," Weatherall said. He arched a smoke ring through circled lips. Dallas was in for another surprise. Before this night was over, the Denver line would be one more step ahead of its competitor.

"How about some coffee?"

"Good idea."

Dallas knelt down, poured a cup, handed it to Weatherall. After filling a second cup, Dallas got to his feet. "It doesn't feel right, us being on different sides."

"No, it doesn't."

"I appreciate your letting me keep that gun."

"I know what it means to you. I feel the same way about that Henry you gave me when I made probation."

"As I recall you could drive nails at twenty yards with a rifle."

"I usually hit what I aim at."

"That's a fact. Your only problem was speed. That is, with a handgun."

"I'm still alive, so I must have been fast enough."

"You never faced a real gunslinger, Creed."

"I faced Buck Weaton."

"I've never understood how you beat Buck. You're not that fast. I'm not even sure I am."

Weatherall shrugged, sipped his coffee. It was hot, black, and strong, and it warmed him. The fire felt good, too. His clothes were still damp, and the night air chilled him. He understood what Dallas was saying, but it didn't bother him. Dallas was running a bluff. He would never pull a gun on Creed. They'd been too close. Dallas owed him too much. Despite all the talk, there'd be no gunplay. Things would continue as they were, each of them trying to stay one jump ahead of the other. Tonight, Dallas was one step behind.

Water splashed as men hurled rails into the river. Somewhere to the east a coyote howled. Jim had found some coal oil and dashed it over the stack of ties. He struck a match, and flames shot up the stacked pilings. The burning wood pulled everyone's attention in that direction, and the Denver crew grinned in satisfaction. As Ace and the other guards half-turned to watch the fire, a subtle expression changed the faces of the Colorado hard cases backed against the wagon. Weatherall said, "Ace, get your mind on your business," and was relieved to see the features of the gang by the wagon go blank. Again he thought of how he hated to leave for main camp. None of his people had ever handled anything like this. He just prayed they were up to it, because he had a job down the line.

Weatherall finished his coffee, set the cup on the ground. "Dallas, I need to borrow a horse."

Dallas's lids drew down. The tip of his tongue touched his upper lip. "Take mine."

Weatherall nodded. "Thanks. Tom, keep

things under control until I get back."

The hands of Weatherall's American Horologe pointed at midnight when he rode into main camp. He snapped the gold case shut, dropped the watch into his vest pocket, then tied his mount to a Denver corral post. He would have to recross the river to reach the Colorado lot, but he had feared to ride up near the opposition's headquarters because hoofbeats might alert the guards. Earlier in the evening, he had checked the Colorado camp and noted that two men had been posted near the barn and corral, with two more patrolling the maintenance area. After blowing the Denver rails, Adams expected some kind of reprisal, so he had set his watchdogs both here and at the end of the tracks.

Ten minutes later, Weatherall lay flat on his belly on the south side of the Arkansas River. Coal-oil lanterns burned alongside the work train. Two more brightened the area around Adams's personal coach. Two lanterns marked the position of the corral guards, while flickering lamplight traced the movement of the two-man patrol.

Shivering in the fifty-five-degree temperature, Weatherall considered his plan. He would have to skirt the Colorado camp, then keep watch from the rear until he'd timed the patrol. Once it was out of range, he would slip into the maintenance shop, steal two five-gallon cans of coal oil, and set fire to the ties stacked behind the shop. Without railroad ties, the Colorado line was out of business until they could import some from Pueblo, and he planned to blow out several sections of Colorado track east of here tomorrow night. That meant Adams would have to haul ties overland by wagon, which would be a slow job.

It took him twenty minutes to reach the rear of the Colorado area, where he dug in behind a clump of juniper. Its pleasant, cedary smell filled his nostrils, and the soft loamy soil made an excellent hiding place. He could see the two guards fronting the corral. The shop lay fifty or sixty yards to his right, and the stacked ties formed solid blocks about ten yards behind it. Once the foot patrol passed, he would sneak into the maintenance shop.

Flickering light marked the walkers as they swung along in front of the work train. They would continue east until they reached the end of the perimeter, where they would turn south around the shop building, past the stacks of ties and rails, then west past the transportation area and the barn. One right turn would carry them back to the work train where their tour would be repeated.

Weatherall laid his chin on crossed forearms. He couldn't time the patrol because it was too dark to see the hands of his watch. He would have to count out their progress. When the two made their southward turn, he started counting. He continued until they hiked past him, reached the barn, and wheeled around it. Then he sprang to his feet and raced across the empty ground between the junipers and the three lines of wagons. There he paused and, using the wagons as a screen, surveyed the area. Two reddish flares silhouetted the two men fronting the corral. Swinging hand-held lanterns marked the two mobile guards, who had reached the work train.

Sliding along the protecting wagons, Weatherall reached a spot opposite the shop, then dashed across empty space into the shop's shadowy outline. His breath came harder than it should have, and his heart lifted and fell in sharp echoes. Despite the chill, sweat beaded his face and upper body. He felt his way down the wall, found a door, and eased into the building. It was darker than outside, so he closed his eyes and stayed put until he had counted to fifty.

When his eyes opened, he could distinguish the dim outlines of machinery and equipment. The place smelled of grease and oily rags, and he heard a rat squeak in a far corner. Light flashed through one of the windows, and he flattened behind a table as the patrol trudged past the shop. They were moving faster than he'd anticipated, or else he'd lost count. He had to be more careful. Once he located the coal oil, he needed time to soak the ties, light the fire, and escape into the darkness. His plans did not include a gunfight.

He located the coal oil stacked against the east wall, and hefting two cans, he eased back to the doorway. He stepped outside and huddled against the building. The walkers had reached the spur track, and the other two men still stood near the corral area. He would have to wait until the patrol passed again because it would take time to wet down the ties. They had to be thoroughly soaked, so they would burn too fast to give the Colorado crew any opportunity to douse the blaze. If he poured the coal oil on now, the guards would be too close when he lit the fires. That would mean he'd have to shoot his way out of here.

Night air flowed around the shop. A pungent odor reached out from the juniper stands. Stars made flickering pinpoints in the domelike sky, and a mule brayed loudly in the barn. That sudden sound breaking across the quiet night startled everyone. Weatherall saw the men at the corral exchange glances, whereupon one of them picked up a lantern and spun toward the barn. The patrol heeled cautiously around, took a long look, then continued their tour. Weatherall's heart had settled into a quick rhythm. His throat was dry, and his damp shirt lay cold against his flesh. This was taking too long.

Fifteen minutes later, the watch scuffed past him, and the moment they turned by the barn, he sprang into action. He trotted up and down the piles of wooden ties, trying to keep in the shadows as he splashed coal oil. He circled the stacks, dumping oil over the ties as he worked his way back to the shop area. As he rounded the ties, a voice yelled, "There's something moving near the rear of the lot."

Footsteps hammered the ground, and Weatherall glanced over his shoulder to see the corral guards running in his direction. With a muffled curse, he flung the remaining oil on the ties and tossed the can aside. When the can hit the shop with a metallic clang, Weatherall cursed again. The guards had circled the corral and rapidly closed the distance. At the same time, light flickering around the barn's corner warned Weatherall that the foot patrol was circling back toward him.

Coal oil's grainy odor penetrated Weatherall's nostrils. He struck a match and held it to the timbers; a yellow-blue blaze ignited. A yell he didn't understand reached him, and he stepped into the shadows between the shop and the ties to strike another match. Coal oil ignited slowly, and he had to get enough fires going so that the wind would whip them into a conflagration. Someone fired a six-gun. Lead splintered wood to Weatherall's right; he half-turned, to see a long-legged figure break from behind one of the wagons. That man's arm straightened, and Weatherall felt the heat as a bullet zipped past his head to dig into the railroad ties. Despite his sense of regret, his hand dipped to his holster, and as his revolver cleared leather, he squeezed off a round that knocked the long-legged fellow backward.

Lights flashed along the work train. Men shouted. Under one of the cars, a dog yelped as half-dressed railroaders tumbled out. A voice cried, "He got Wes." Weatherall bit into his upper lip. He had to light more fires. Once they flared, the breeze would whip them into a wall of flame. He triggered another round into the wagons, then dashed down the stacks, pausing to light fires along the way. Angry yells lifted over the area. Somewhere a cowbell clanged, and the sharp odor of burning oil swept the yard. The wind fed the flames, whose yellowish glow illuminated the yard while the burnt-cork odor of smoke layered the area.

Weatherall's heart thudded against his chest. He felt hot. Sticky. A squat man broke into the clear near the west end of the burning ties, but he ducked to cover before Weatherall could squeeze the trigger. Weatherall reached the stack's east corner. Beyond lay the cover of the darkened plateau. All he had to do was reach that darkness, and he was safe. Flames devoured the ties. Thick black smoke filled the sky. Men yelled, screamed, cursed, and somewhere to Weatherall's right a gun exploded. His job was finished. It was time to move. One quick sprint would carry him beyond the lighted area, to safety. Yet some vague warning held him. He'd heard nothing. Seen nothing. But some primitive sixth sense rang a deep-seated alarm.

The footsteps of moving men swept up to him. He sensed danger closing from every side. He had to break for it. Still, the dryness of his palate, the chill on his backbone, the cramp in his gut told him danger lay beyond the rapidly retreating shadows. The flames leaped higher. Gunshots boomed and lead thudded into burning timber. Danger was a smell. A sound. A taste. All his animal instincts surfaced and pushed reason aside.

The yelling closed on him. Men darted

between the wagons. As red streaks flared from fired revolvers, and lead whined around him, Weatherall swung out around the pilings, six-gun at the ready. When he moved into open ground a red dart streaked the darkness twenty feet upwind, and something tugged at his vest. As a gunshot ripped the night Weatherall lined his sights on the Colorado hand's midsection. The gun bucked against Weatherall's palm twice, and the man fronting him dropped like a cut rope.

Then Weatherall was behind the firelight's glow. With the darkness enveloping him, he circled the panicked Colorado camp to recross the river. Upon reaching the north side, he sagged into a crosslegged position to catch his breath. Across the river bedlam prevailed. The noise and confusion had awakened the Denver crew, who talked in mystified tones alongside their sleeping quarters. Weatherall shivered in the cold breeze. A sickness churned his gut as an unpleasant knowledge hammered through him: He'd killed two men tonight.

Those dead men would pile pressure on Dallas Mason, because he had to prove he was tougher than Creed Weatherall. Otherwise, Dallas would lose face, the one thing he couldn't afford. Dallas's business was an eye for an eye, and tonight had put his reputation on the table. Weatherall shook his head. He muttered some words that made him feel as though his mouth should be washed out with soap. He'd started a shooting war. The last thing he wanted.

CHAPTER 9

Just before sunrise, Weatherall and his crew arrived in the main camp. After burning the Colorado ties, he had gathered a string of mounts from the Denver line and ridden to the track end, where he'd found things under control. Now the long night was over. The men turned their animals into the corral and headed for the mess tent. Stifling a yawn, Weatherall trudged behind them. He was tired. He had a sore throat, a runny nose, and a headache. As he glanced across the river at the opposite camp, his lips squared at the thought of what had happened over there.

After washing up, he followed his men into the mess tent. It was warm inside, and the full-flavored odor of black coffee hit him. Around the tent, curious railroaders glanced up from their breakfasts. At the tent's far end Charlotte, the colonel, and Will stared at him, and relief flooded Charlotte's lovely face. Weatherall walked up to them, dropped into a chair. He sagged wearily, not even bothering to remove his Stetson. He felt Charlotte's hand on his thigh, and the concern in her eyes brought a lump to his throat.

The colonel's wary gaze appraised him. "What happened across the river?"

Weatherall stuck a cigar between his teeth, brought a match to it. "Everything went sour. I had to shoot a couple of people."

The colonel's jaw dropped. His puffy face looked slimmer. "Did you kill them?"

"I think so."

"Holy cow! All hell's going to break loose."

Charlotte poured a cup of steaming coffee and set it before Weatherall. "You sound terrible. Do you want something to eat?"

"Coffee will be fine."

Charlotte squeezed his shoulder. "You mustn't feel guilty. You didn't want to kill those men. You did what you had to do."

He sipped the hot coffee, felt the heat settle through his body. The men who had accompanied him sat at a separate table from their fellow workers. They ate without talking. He sensed a quiet fear among them; he'd explained what had happened. Now they worried about what was certain to come. He glanced at the colonel, who had pushed his plate away and was staring at the table. Concern furrowed the colonel's heavy brow, and his left hand unconsciously tapped the table. Will chewed on a biscuit, his thoughts obviously elsewhere.

Sunrise reddened the tent's east flaps. A wren sang his morning song. The colonel's gaze lifted to Weatherall. "What happens now?"

"Dallas has to even the score."

Charlotte touched Weatherall's arm. "You mean more killings?"

"I can't see it any other way."

The colonel placed his elbows on the table and laid his head in his palms. Will choked on his biscuit, hurriedly gulped some coffee. Charlotte nervously studied her husband. Weatherall sniffed. He cleared his scratchy throat. He felt feverish. His head pounded, and he wiped his runny nose with a handkerchief.

Will poured coffee into his mug, refilled the other three mugs. "I guess we all expected something like this when Adams sent for Dallas Mason."

Weatherall cleared his throat again. "Dallas didn't kill anybody. I did."

"Yeah, but nothing like this happened until he arrived."

Charlotte's full lips parted. Her eyes darkened. "I knew all along you were lying. Otherwise you wouldn't have come back from Raton Pass without your hat. Now what really happened down there?"

186

"It was a setup. I was lucky to get out alive. But Dallas wasn't even on the scene yet."

The colonel snorted. "Why do you always defend that man?"

"We were friends. I know him."

"You only know what he used to be. You refuse to recognize what he has become."

"Dallas doesn't want any killing any more than I do."

"Then why did you say there'd be more of it?"

"Colonel, I went out last night to even the score. He's got to do the same."

Charlotte lit one of her thin cigars as a grim fatalism paled her cheeks. "Then we have to get even . . . and this goes on and on. Creed, can't you see where this is leading?"

"We'll hit them. They'll hit us. Right now we're ahead, and I intend to keep it that way."

Weatherall felt Charlotte's gaze settle on the side of his face. "You're going to have to stand up to Dallas."

"It won't come to that."

"It has to come to that."

"If Dallas wanted that kind of trouble, he would have called me out the day he arrived. I know the man, Charlotte. It won't happen."

The smoke from her cigar stung his ballooned-up nostrils. He cleared his throat and swallowed some coffee. His eyes burned from fatigue. The colonel slurped his coffee while Will fiddled with his case knife. Weatherall wiped his nose. He glanced at his wife. She was scared but trying hard not to show it. It was her way of saying she was behind him all the way.

The colonel set his tin mug on the table. "What I can't figure is what you hoped to gain by burning those ties across the river."

"Simple. Without ties, they can't make track."

"They'll just freight some in from Pueblo."

"Not after I blow out a section of rail east of here tonight."

The colonel's eyes sobered. He shook his head. "It's going to be like this from now on, isn't it?"

"Until one of us reaches Canon City."

Will fired up his pipe. "They can't move without ties."

"So now they'll hit our main camp," the colonel said.

Weatherall grunted. "They'll try. We're going to have to have four or five men guarding that compound. Those ties are our edge."

The colonel nodded. "You're right. By the time they wagon those ties in from Pueblo, we'll be eight or ten days ahead of them. That is, if they don't . . ."

Weatherall rubbed his eyes. He was tired

of talk. He wanted to go to bed. But he sensed the colonel's agitation. The man was a born worrier. He was afraid of what Dallas might do, and he didn't want to sit here and think about it alone. Weatherall picked up a biscuit, spread some butter on it. He wasn't hungry, but common sense told him to put something in his stomach. He hadn't eaten for over twelve hours.

Charlotte leaned over and whispered in his ear. "You look exhausted. Why don't we go home?"

He smiled and shook his head. Her eyes told him she understood, and he experienced the rush of pride he always felt when she was near him. Even at this early hour, she was so beautiful, so poised, so full of life. He would never get over the joy of knowing she belonged to him.

A match flared as the colonel lit a cigar. Talk flowed around the tent, and tension thickened the atmosphere. The crew had heard about last night's activity. They wondered what came next.

Charlotte pushed her chair back from the table. She stood up. "Creed, you're worn out. Let's go home and get a couple of shots of bourbon into you. Then I'll give you a rubdown. You need some sleep if you're working tonight."

★ ★ ★

Two days later Weatherall walked into their coach to find Charlotte sewing a button on his gray shirt. "I'm riding out to the end of the tracks to see how things are progressing. Want to go?"

She laid the sewing aside and glanced out the window. "Looks like a beautiful day for a ride."

"Thought you'd feel that way. Hank's got a couple of horses saddled and waiting."

Ten minutes later they followed the tracks west. The sun warmed their backs. A dry breeze cooled the morning. They rode at a trot, the horses' hooves sending up sodden echoes from the loamy soil. The plateau rose in a gentle incline, a continuing lift from around four thousand feet at Pueblo to a little over five thousand at Canon City. Far to the north, scavengers circled, but they were only dots in a cloudless sky. Except for the hoofbeats, the only sound was the jingle of metal, the squeak of saddle leather.

Charlotte reached out to touch Weatherall's arm. "I'm glad you asked me."

"So am I. We don't spend enough time together."

"We spend a lot of time together."

"Well, it's not enough."

"I don't say it very often, but I love you,

Creed Weatherall."

"I love you, too."

"We've had a good life together."

"Better than good."

"Creed, I've never mentioned this before, but . . . Creed, every woman wants a child."

He glanced over at her as his brow crinkled. "I'm sorry. I never even suspected."

"I know a railroad camp's a poor place to raise a baby. But do you mind?"

"If that's what you want, that's what I want."

"I've been wanting to say something. I just didn't know how to."

He glanced back to the front. The tip of his tongue pressed his upper right molars as he stared into the distance. After a few moments, he stuck a cigar between his teeth, brought a match to it. "Charlotte, a lot of men have families, but their families are back in Denver. I think that'd be best for us. I don't want a baby of mine brought up around a hell-on-wheels camp."

"Creed, I can't leave you."

"It wouldn't be for long. Then I'll find some other kind of work. Something more stable."

"You wouldn't like that. You're not the kind to be tied to one spot."

"Then it's time I changed. A family man's got to be responsible."

"I'm sorry I said anything. I think —"

Up ahead a horseman galloped toward them. A lone figure waved his hat wildly while a yell funneled over the prairie. "That looks like Dave," Creed said. "He's supposed to be with the work crew."

They kicked their horses into action, and as the distance narrowed, Dave's honest features came into focus. Dust billowed behind as he pulled up to them. "Mason and his boys were laying for us. At least two dead and one wounded. I'm headed back for more men."

"Where did this happen?" Creed said.

"About four miles up track. We were lucky. If it hadn't been for those ties, there'd be more dead."

"I'll head out there. Charlotte, you go back to camp with Dave."

"I'm going with you."

Weatherall's lips rolled back in an exasperated grimace. "Woman, sometimes you are impossible. Well, there's no time to argue. Dave, get the boys back on the double. Come on, Charlotte."

The shooting abruptly stopped when Weatherall and Charlotte galloped up to the stalled work train. They drew rein at the train's south side so that they were protected from the Colorado gunmen dug in to the northwest. A harried Colonel Thompson rushed out to meet them. His hat had fallen off; his gray hair was rumpled. "Did Dave get through?"

"He's on his way back to camp," Weatherall said, as he and Charlotte dismounted. "How are things?"

"Not good. Two men dead. One wounded. Charlotte, you shouldn't be here."

"We both know that," Weatherall said.

The colonel led the way to a flatcar where the men had hastily dumped ties and made a fort out of those remaining aboard. They'd climbed up into the car, where they slumped down behind the wooden barrier. Eight other men crouched behind the heavy ties, and sweat not caused by the sun filmed their set countenances. A man lay in the far corner. His chest lifted unevenly; blood colored his shirt.

Weatherall put a hand on Charlotte's shoulder. "Joel's been hit. Scoot over and see if you can do anything to make him comfortable."

As she crawled off, Weatherall considered the layout. Sometime during early morning, the Colorado gang had set up behind a sandstone ridge running north and south. Otherwise, this area was flat land, which offered no protection. Dallas had picked the spot with his usual care. If this train hadn't been carrying ties, the Denver crew would have been ducks in a shooting gallery. Weatherall spotted a figure sprawled facedown in the dirt near the cab. He had to be Hobie Mix, the engineer. Hobie had had a wife and three children back in Denver; they were a fine, close-knit family, and Weatherall was glad it was the colonel who had to write the widow.

"Wonder why they stopped shooting?" the colonel said.

"Probably so they wouldn't hit me and Charlotte when we rode in."

"I forgot. Mason's perfectly willing to kill the rest of us, but he won't hurt you." With a snort, the colonel turned to the front.

Weatherall fired up a cigar and considered the situation. They could be holed up here for hours. Dallas couldn't get to them behind this thick barrier of ties, and they didn't dare rush Dallas until Dave returned with reinforcements. Weatherall glanced right, to where Charlotte wiped the sweat from Joel's forehead with a cloth. Joel needed a doctor, but the closest one was ten miles from here. Weatherall studied the frightened faces of the other men trapped on the flatcar. He knew them all. They were workingmen, not fighting men; still, they would stick it out. That said a lot for them.

Weatherall swung around to the colonel. "I'm going to have a talk with Dallas."

"About what?"

"Joel's in bad shape. I'll try to talk Dallas into calling this off, so we can get Joel back to camp."

The colonel threw Weatherall a wall-eyed look. "You're wasting your time."

"Maybe." Weatherall cupped his hands to his lips. "Dallas, this is Creed. I want to talk."

After about ten seconds, Dallas called out. "So we talk."

Weatherall glanced at Charlotte, who looked alarmed. He winked at her, climbed atop the ties, and leaped to the ground. As his boots hit dirt, Dallas stepped around the sandstone and met him halfway between the ridge and the train.

"Looks like a standoff," Weatherall said.

"It does at that."

"Why don't we call it off?"

"That might look like I'm running. You're still one up on me because of that blown track between here and Pueblo."

"You saw Dave ride out. He'll be back soon with more men. We can overrun you."

Dallas's fingertips caressed the scar puckering his cheek. "That would cost you."

"True. So why push it?"

"Creed, why don't you take Charlotte and

go back to Denver?"

"I can't do it, Dallas."

"What if it comes down to you and me?"

"That'll never happen and you know it."

Dallas shook his head. An angry breath broke from his lips. "Don't you see the spot you're putting me in?"

"I can't help it. I've got to play this out. Now, do we call it off?"

Dallas closed his eyes for a long moment. "You win. But Creed, it's got to come to a head sometime."

"I'll worry about that if it comes."

Dallas gave Weatherall a long stare, then shook his head. Weatherall watched him wheel around and walk back to the sandstone bluff.

CHAPTER 10

When Jim Smith walked into Bullard's Emporium, faces turned in his direction, then tilted quickly away. As he paused just inside the tent flap, voices grew muted and the atmosphere seemed charged and full. The band sawed out a tuneless "Buffalo Gals," and the floor was crowded with Bullard's shady women and their clumsy partners. A roulette wheel clicked hollowly. Lamplight reflected off glass, and someone at the tent's rear, unaware of Jim's entrance hollered, "Sevens!"

Jim lit a cigar, and as he shook out the match, he saw Nelly May standing at the bar. Her head was tipped down so she didn't see him reflected in the fifty-foot mirror. She was more beautiful than he'd remembered, and a familiar longing washed over him. Her partner was a bald-headed man Jim didn't know, and this fellow kept patting her hip, her thigh, her shoulder. Jim looked away, wondering if he was as big a fool as Creed had suggested. But he wanted to see her. Needed to see her.

She was all he ever thought of. He glanced around the room, glad that Tully Williams wasn't present.

Footsteps sounded to Jim's right as Tom Love stepped up beside him. Tom's naturally cheerful face looked somber. "I'm sorry to see you here."

"Felt like dancing."

"And only with her."

"With her."

"Jim, you're the best friend I've got in this camp. Let's drink someplace else."

"I can't, Tom."

Tom swore and pulled at his cap's crinkled brim. "Let's sit down. I'll buy you a drink."

"I want to talk to Nelly May."

"She's already got a client. Now don't cause more trouble than you've already got."

Jim nodded and followed Tom to a table. While Tom ordered drinks, Jim gave the tent a careful appraisal. He saw Sam White, Lee Keene, Will Johnson, but they didn't look at him. Farther back, at the poker table, Jim spotted Dallas Mason, who regarded him curiously before glancing at his cards. Beyond Dallas sat two Colorado men who'd been at the tie-burning party. As Jim turned back to his table, he saw one of Bullard's bouncers striding toward the tent's rear flap.

The waiter set the drinks on the table, took Tom's money, and departed. Jim sipped his drink. It seemed hot in here, but Jim knew it wasn't the surroundings that caused his discomfort. He glanced at the bar, saw Nelly May still chatting with the bald man, and gritted his teeth. He needed to have a few minutes alone with her before Tully arrived.

Across the table, Tom packed his pipe. "You made a mistake coming here."

"Maybe, but it's too late to change things now."

"We can drink somewhere else."

Jim shook his head. "I came here to settle something, Tom. I can't dodge it any longer."

"Jim, are you a complete fool? That woman cares nothing about you. To her, you're just another trick."

"I've never been that."

"Then you *are* a fool. What do you get for your money?"

Jim shrugged. As he puffed his cigar, his attention settled on Amos Bullard cutting through the tent's back flap, followed by a hulking sidekick. Jim swallowed a quick gulp of bourbon as Bullard angled his way. He hoped Bullard wasn't going to order him out, because this thing with Tully had to be settled.

Bullard pulled up at their table. Lamplight

reflected from the heavy gold watch chain crossing his belly, flashed a white sliver from the four-carat diamond on his left hand. "I was hoping we'd seen the last of you."

"Why, Amos, what a thing to say."

"You know what I mean. Look, Jim, I don't want any trouble in here."

"I won't cause any trouble."

"Son, I've been in this business all my life. I know Nelly May's a beautiful woman, but she's just like the rest of them. When she looks at you, she sees a two-dollar gold piece. Believe me, that's all she sees. Now, why don't you leave?"

"I can't."

Bullard's heavy shoulders lifted, fell. He said, "Have it your way," and wheeled toward the front of the tent.

Jim watched Nelly May. He threw down his bourbon and shifted restlessly in his chair, drumming his fingertips against the table. He couldn't horn in at the bar. She might be arranging a . . . He refused to think the word.

The dry, aromatic smell of pipe smoke wafted around him. He shifted his attention to Tom, who regarded him impassively. "Want another drink?"

When the man Nelly May had been talking to walked away, Jim sprang to his feet. He had to get to her before anyone else did.

Nelly May didn't look his way, but she knew he was there. He could tell by the guarded expression that pinched her cheeks. When he eased in beside her, her face seemed to pale under its thick coat of paint.

"You haven't been here for two weeks. Why tonight?"

"I felt like dancing."

"Well, dance somewhere else. Tully's been bragging all over camp how he's run you out of here. He's looking for an excuse to pound you to a pulp, and you're giving it to him."

"Thanks for the vote of confidence."

"Jim, you're no brawler. We both know that."

He scuffed at his nose. His easygoing features stiffened, and his mouth drew down at the corners. "Aren't you even a bit glad to see me?"

"I'm always glad to see anybody with money to spend."

It was hot in the tent. The atmosphere was heavy. Jim found it hard to breathe. He fought to hide his disappointment and drew a steadying draw on his cigar. His gut churned. His head tipped forward. He couldn't look at her. He had to get his emotions under control.

"Jim, why don't you leave while there's still time?"

His head came up. He looked her square in the face. "I missed coming here. I missed talking to you."

All her features loosened, and some emotion he couldn't fathom came over her face. She reached out and touched his forearm as wetness gleamed in her eyes. "Are you crazy? What are you trying to prove?"

"That I'm a man."

"You're a fool. All of you are fools. You think the only way you can be a man is to get your head kicked in. Jim, you have nothing to prove."

"Maybe not to you."

"Then to who? Look around. Notice how quiet this place has become since you walked in. These men like you. They don't want to see you get hurt anymore than I do."

Jim glanced around the tent. The band still played. The dancers moved back and forth across the floor. But the place was strangely hushed. Men talked in whispers and kept their gazes averted. Even the men along the bar stood so that they didn't have to face him. The only person who seemed aware of him was Amos Bullard, who stood near the tent's front flap, flanked by two bull-shouldered goons.

Jim swung back to the bar. "How about that dance?"

"You won't have it any other way, will you?"

"No."

With a sigh, she turned toward the dance floor with Jim following. Even in this closed-off space filled with cheap whiskey odors, strong tobacco, and unwashed men, when he took her in his arms the springlike fragrance of her hair enclosed him, while the heady scent of her musky perfume raised his heartbeat. Her cheeks lay soft against his as her full-bodied figure followed his every move. The strength of how much he had missed her formed a lump in his throat, and his arms tightened around her.

Her body was tense, rigid, and he suddenly realized that although he was enjoying the dance, her movements were strictly mechanical. His thoughts might be on her, but hers were elsewhere. Her steps were as precise and automatic as a wound-up doll's. Pulling back, he looked down at her, but she refused to meet his gaze. After a moment, he pulled her close. If he was going to get his head beat in over her, he might as well enjoy it. As they swayed to the beat, he felt despair. Loneliness. Misgivings. Why was he here? Why was he doing this? Everyone thought he was a fool. Even Nelly May.

Nelly May pulled to a halt. "I can't dance

anymore." He stepped back, looked down at her. Her flesh stretched tightly over her cheekbones; her lips were very red and very thin.

He shrugged. "We'll have a drink, then."

Her shoulders sagged. The corners of her lips drew down as she gazed off beyond his right shoulder. "Maybe this *is* the only way."

Signaling the waiter for drinks, Jim led her off the dance floor to a nearby table. The waiter brought the drinks and Jim lifted his glass to Nelly May. "It's good seeing you again."

Her eyes shot toward the tent flap, and her upper lip curled. A warning. Jim heard boots pound the dirt floor. He felt the tension sweeping out from the tables around them. His heart hit the top of his mouth as sweat popped out across his shoulders.

Tully wheeled up before them. His thick lips broke into a menacing smile. "You made a mistake coming here tonight. I thought I'd made it clear I didn't want you hanging around Bullard's."

The tent was dead quiet. Along the bar, men kept their backs turned, their attention strictly on their drinks. At the surrounding tables, men sat with lowered heads. The roulette wheel fluttered to a stop, and when someone accidentally dropped a coin on a table everyone jerked involuntarily.

Tully reached out and grabbed Jim's shirt front. "It's time I taught you a lesson."

"Not now, Tully," Nelly May said. "I don't think Amos would like it."

Tully's head swiveled toward the tent's flap. His jawline twitched, but he released Jim's shirt. "You'll be leaving. So will I. Come on, Nelly May. Let's get a drink."

An iron taste rusted Jim's tongue, and he felt blood pounding in his ears. His heart felt as if it would burst through his chest. "Nelly May's drinking with me." Jim pushed to his feet, looked out at the crowd. "Men, at ten tomorrow, I'll be waiting for Tully out beyond the corral. That is, if he's got the backbone to show up."

Tully rubbed his hands together. "Don't worry. I'll be there. You enjoy your whiskey, sonny. It will be the last you ever drink with those teeth in place." With a sneer, Tully heeled to the bar.

Jim sank into his chair. He glanced at the men around him, but they didn't look back. His insides felt watery, and when he looked down at his hands, they were shaking. He knew that his voice had sounded loud, unnatural. He also knew that these men understood that he was afraid, and he felt ashamed that he had not been able to hide his emotions.

Well, the thing was done. He had to play it out.

Nelly May stared at him, her trained features hiding all feeling. Her hands touched the table, fell to her lap, then lifted to the table again. Her blue eyes were as blank as a glass of water. "I hope you're satisfied."

Jim gulped down his bourbon, tried to light a cigar, but he couldn't hold the match still. "I looked a fool, didn't I?"

"You are a fool. What do you possibly hope to gain from this stupidity?"

He stared at his unlit cigar, shrugged. "I'm not sure myself. I guess I'll be going."

When he stood up, her gaze followed him. One hand touched her throat, and tiny rivers carved her cheeks. She said, "I'm so sorry," and after giving him one mute stare wheeled abruptly toward the tent's rear flap.

Jim found himself standing outside Bullard's main tent. He felt as drained as an empty canteen, and he stared out across the street without really seeing anything. He regretted not being able to carry it off better, but a man did the best he could. At least he hadn't shown yellow. As for Nelly May, he completely failed to comprehend her final reaction. But, then, he'd never been able to understand her.

"You'd better get a good night's sleep.

You're going to need it."

Jim half-turned to meet Tom Love's distraught gaze. "I think I'll go get drunk. Want to join me?"

"No, thanks. The last thing you need tomorrow is a hangover."

Jim Smith clasped his hands and glanced around the circle of men surrounding the area beyond the corral. About seventy-five people were gathered here, awaiting the fight. For the most part they were quiet and gloomy, which was a surprise. Jim had witnessed a few fistfights, and the crowds had always bubbled with expectation. Most men loved a good fight. Particularly in a boring, godforsaken camp such as this. Perhaps that was the problem. They didn't expect this one to last long enough to make it interesting.

Jim's mouth tried to work up some moisture. He glanced at Weatherall and said, "He's late."

"He's trying to make you sweat. It's an old trick."

"I'm too dried up to sweat."

"That's natural. Don't worry about it."

A hand fell on Jim's shoulder, and he turned to look into George Duncan's sober features. "We're all behind you, son. Remember when Dallas stopped those wagons? Tully didn't act so tough then. Lay into him. He's got a yellow streak."

Jim nodded as George faded into the crowd. Back at the wagons, they'd faced gunplay. Tully had never pretended to be a gunfighter, but that didn't diminish his reputation as a brawler.

A flock of magpies flew up from their feeding. A slight breeze ruffled Jim's hair. His stomach felt constricted, and his heart beat a savage tattoo in his throat. He had the strange sensation of standing outside his body. It was as though he had split in two. One part, the flesh and blood part, waited here for Tully. The other part, the intellectual part, circled beyond like an indifferent stranger. Jim licked his lips, hoping the others didn't see the fear he masked behind his stolid face. He'd never been in a fight. What would he do the first time Tully hit him? Could he handle the pain? Would he go down? Would he run? God, he wished Tully would arrive. The fight would be hell; however, nothing could be worse than this waiting.

The smoke from Weatherall's cigar reached him, and Weatherall's hand closed over his shoulder. "Believe me, you'll do fine."

"What if I can't stand up to him?"

"It's no disgrace to lose a fight, but let's be positive. Remember what I taught you.

Tully knows you're afraid. He means to play with you. That's your advantage. He'll be expecting you to move away from him. Instead, you'll bore right in. You've got to get inside, push your head into his chest, then go for his midsection. You've got to stay inside. Otherwise, he'll cut you to pieces."

Jim grunted, glanced nervously around the circle of muttering men. He felt as if his bowels were going to drop right out of his bottom, and his mouth was so dry it hurt.

Weatherall's grip tightened on Jim's shoulder. "Remember. Forget his head. He's got a jaw as strong as a piece of track. Hit him in the gut. That's where you'll win your fight."

An abrupt silence fell over the crowd. Jim glanced right and saw Tully swagger through an alley that had opened as men parted before him. Tully's mean little eyes hooded as their gaze met, and a smile tugged at Tully's meaty lips. When the alley closed behind him, he stood flat-footed, glaring across the ring unblinkingly. Jim fought to hold that stare. He turned cold. Hot. Cold again. The ring seemed to have shrunk to the size of a barrel, and he felt trapped, helpless. He'd never considered himself a coward, but now he wondered. He couldn't hold Tully's gaze, and when his chin dipped, Tully snickered.

Jim glanced up to find Tully removing his shirt. Tully's body gleamed porcelain white in contrast to his bronzed face, neck, and hands. Muscles rippled across his shoulders and chest. "Ready to dance?"

Jim's Adam's apple caught in his throat. He didn't answer because he knew his voice would quaver, but he nodded.

Tully grinned. He strolled across the ring, not even bothering to lift his guard. Jim stiffened at Tully's contempt. He obviously wasn't expecting much of a fight. Jim glanced at Weatherall, who winked, and Jim brought his arms up, elbows and fists close together the way Weatherall had taught him. Tully's arrogant approach touched some deep-seated primordial instinct deep in Jim. That fear became a weapon that honed all his senses. Suddenly, he was more keenly aware of every sight and smell and sound than he had ever been in his life. All his nerve endings tingled, and he knew no matter what happened, he wouldn't break.

As Tully closed, a burst of energy ripped Jim's sturdy frame. When he flung himself violently forward, he caught the amazed dilation of Tully's black eyes. Caught off-guard, Tully still managed to slam an awkward right into Jim's mouth.

Jim felt his lips split against his teeth. Blood

salted his tongue, and his head roared. He bucked ahead as a wild exhaltation fueled him. He'd been hit. He'd tasted his own blood. But he was still on his feet, and he had walked through Tully's fist and found himself inside Tully's powerful arms. Jim's fear fell away as he pushed his head into Tully's chest. He slammed a right hook into Tully's stomach, then hammered a wicked left into the same spot. Tully's arms flailed wildly but Jim was in too close for those blows to carry any power.

Tully stepped back in an effort to open the distance, but Jim surged ahead and his fists battered Tully's unprotected belly. Tully tried to push Jim away with open hands, and Jim brought an uppercut from the ground. It sank under Tully's ribcage. Tully gasped. His face turned as white as his body, and his mouth gasped for air.

Jim felt a wildness he'd never known. He'd landed a liver shot, and Creed had told him that a liver shot practically paralyzed a man. Tully was his.

A voice screeched, "You've got him," and another man yelled, "Kill him! Kill him!" A blaze of confidence shot through Jim's body, and all the insults he'd taken from Tully over the months fueled a new anger. Jim forgot what he was supposed to do. How he'd been told to finish this. Instead of stepping inside, he hurled a right across at Tully's jaw, followed by a left jab at Tully's right eye.

Tully took the blow square on the chin, then shifted left. Jim's fist dug through empty space. Lumbering forward, Tully wrapped his arms around Jim and held him in a bear hug. Jim tried to work Tully's body as Tully leaned against him, resting, waiting for the pain to subside. Jim hit Tully in the side, the back, the top of the head, but Tully held on. Jim's exhilaration turned to despair as he felt Tully's arms tighten. One stupid mistake had turned this affair around.

Abruptly, Tully's arms unlocked. He stepped back and drove a right into Jim's chin. As Tully's left crashed against Jim's forehead, his world whirled, and the ground slammed into his back. He stared up into a red mist to find Tully staring down at him. He watched Tully's boot lift, saw the heavy sole positioned directly over his chest. In a world that closed and receded, Weatherall's sharp "Tully!" dribbled into Jim's consciousness. The uplifted boot paused, then faded away. Jim rolled to his side. His head hurt. The inside of his mouth felt swollen. His legs and arms wouldn't work right. Somewhere someone mumbled, "Get up. Get up," and he dimly understood the words fell from his

212

own battered lips.

Somehow he reached his feet. He locked his knees so that he wouldn't fall, but before he could raise his hundred-pound arms, Tully's fist smashed into his face. Jim hit the ground. Pain stitched his entire body. His world was gray. He could see nothing but blurs as dim sounds filtered into his plugged ears. He rolled to his stomach, painfully pushed up to his knees, and finally staggered to his feet. As he fought to maintain his balance, a fist buried itself in his temple, and the world turned black.

. . . Dampness sponged Jim's brow. Moisture streaked his cheeks, and his eyes fluttered open to focus on Weatherall. Behind Weatherall's huge shoulders loomed Tom Love's worried countenance. Jim tried to get up, but Weatherall pushed him back as he wiped Jim's face with a wet cloth. Tom grunted, removed the corncob from his teeth. "He's finally come to. Jim, you've been out around ten minutes. You okay?"

"I think so." He started to sit up, and this time when Weatherall pushed him back, pain shot from the tip of his chin to the top of his skull. He suddenly felt sick. He gritted his teeth against the nausea working up from his belly.

Leaving the damp cloth on Jim's forehead,

Weatherall leaned back. "You'll be all right. Nothing broken. Just lie there a minute. You were lucky."

"Damn lucky," Tom grunted. "I hope you're a hell of a lover because you'll never be a fighter."

"Was I that bad?"

Weatherall chuckled. "Not really. You just lost your head. You had him and you let him get away. We call that lacking the killer instinct. But you don't have to worry about Tully. You gave him a lot more than he wanted. I'm proud of you."

Jim closed his eyes. The nausea receded, but the top of his skull was about to blow off. His lips felt the size of sausages, and his teeth ached. But he'd made it. He'd held on to the finish. He didn't want to fight anyone ever again; still, it hadn't been as bad as he'd feared. "Can I get up now?"

"I think so. Just take it easy."

With Weatherall's help, Jim wobbled to his feet. He was tired. So tired. He had trouble keeping his balance, but with Weatherall's help stumbled toward the boarding car.

CHAPTER 11

Creed Weatherall pushed back from the table and looked across its flat surface to the colonel's satisfied face. They'd spent the past hour working out the logistical details of making track through the gorge. They'd talked about rails, ties, support crews, and other details that didn't interest Weatherall a whole hell of a lot. But it was part of the job, so he gave it as much attention as any other part of the work.

The colonel lit a cigar, shook out the match. "You know, I can't believe we're only twenty miles from Canon City. Creed, we're going to make it."

"That's what I've been telling you."

"You know me. If there's no problem, I'll invent one. But there is one question. How much longer is Adams going to sit back and let us build? What about your friend Mason? He's not earning his money."

"We're armed and ready, Colonel. You might say we're holding the high ground. At this point, Dallas wouldn't come off too well in a direct attack."

The colonel checked his watch. "Eight-thirty. Too early even for me to drink. How's Jim feeling?"

"Got some cuts and bruises. But he's working."

"After that licking he took yesterday, he should have rested a day or two."

"I agree, but he's out to prove something."

"He's proved it. I hated to miss that fight, but in my position I couldn't afford to be there. I'm going over to the mess tent for some coffee. Want to join me?"

"No thanks. I promised Charlotte I'd look at her mare today. She needs some shoes. I want to be sure Costello gets it right. 'Lazy' is his middle name."

Weatherall followed the colonel from the coach. As his boss headed for the mess hall, Weatherall crossed his arms over his chest and stared west. Charlotte had gone out with the work train today. Dub Beach had the fever, so she'd volunteered to take his place with the mess crew. She was a woman who liked to stay busy. There wasn't much to keeping their coach comfortable, and there wasn't that much mail. So she found other outlets for her energy. Again he realized how lucky he was to have found her. There were a lot of women, but only one Charlotte.

Weatherall swung west to find a rider bearing in to camp. As the distance closed, hoofbeats drummed down to him, and the silhouette turned into Jim Smith. Alarm struck Weatherall's chest. Jim had gone out with the work train. Only trouble could bring him back at this time of day.

The big roan roared up to him. Jim reined the horse in and dropped to the ground. Pain and grief twisted his swollen face. His mouth opened and closed involuntarily. "There's been a bad wreck. We've got to get some equipment up there."

Weatherall grabbed Jim's shoulder. "Charlotte! What about my wife?"

Jim's gaze dropped off to one side. He swallowed hard. "She's dead."

"Dead! What are you talking about? What happened?"

"Creed, I'm sorry. There was no other way to say it. The train jumped the track. Flipped over. Most of us were thrown free. We were all right. But . . . Charlotte. She broke her neck."

Weatherall's big hands dropped to his sides. He fought back a rising panic. It was a mistake. It had to be a mistake.

"Creed, I've got to find the colonel."

"He's in the mess tent."

As Jim wheeled away, Weatherall stood

rooted. He didn't want to think about it. He wouldn't think about it. Charlotte was hurt and he had to get help. The others! He hadn't even asked about the others. And what had gone wrong? Why had the train jumped the track? The colonel's "Your friend isn't earning his money" blazed across Weatherall's brain, and his hands closed into hammers. He glanced downriver toward the Colorado camp. He'd never wanted any trouble with Dallas, but if it was true . . . if Charlotte was hurt . . .

A voice caught his attention, and he found the colonel facing him, flanked by Jim Smith. "Creed, I'm sorry about Charlotte, but there's no time to mourn. We've got to get a hoist engine out to that wreck. Steve Jenkins and Vic Lord are trapped under the locomotive. We've got to lift it. Holy cow! I hope they're not dead already. I'm sending Jim to round up what men he can find. You and I'd better get over to the shop. Again, I'm sorry about Charlotte."

"Charlotte's all right."

"But Jim said —"

"Jim made a mistake."

The colonel shot Weatherall a guarded glance, cut his eyes to Jim, nodded. "Right. Now let's get moving." The colonel's chubby features tensed with strain as he grabbed

Weatherall's elbow. "Let's get going, son."

Before the work train grated to a stop, Weatherall's feet hit the ground. To his right, flatcars lay strewn like broken toys while beyond, the engine lay on one side, its cowcatcher buried in soil. The odors of steam and oil and scorched metal mingled pungently. Some men stood in shock. Some tended the wounded. Some formed work gangs to try to pry up the smashed locomotive. Dick Reisman rushed by Weatherall, who reached out to grab his shirtfront. "Where's Charlotte?"

Reisman blinked. His fingers fumbled with his reddish beard as he pointed off to the left. "Over there."

Weatherall's eyes followed Dick's finger, and a dull burning shot up through his chest. His hand fell from Dick's shirt, and the next thing he knew he was kneeling by his wife. An unnatural pallor dyed her complexion. Her neck lay at an awkward angle. Weatherall felt something break in the middle of his breast, and he shuddered. He reached down and picked up her hand. It was cold. He'd never felt such coldness. He stared at her face, his vision blurred; salt embittered his lips. Something caught in his throat, and he looked away from her. He wanted to scream. To yell. To hurt someone. To do something, anything, to dull the agony ripping him apart. Time faded. The world faded, and when it came back, he realized he was still holding her hand.

He glanced around to see that the colonel had positioned the hoist engine. Men attached cables to the overturned locomotive in preparation to free the two men trapped under the tonnage. Wearily, Weatherall crossed Charlotte's hands over her breast. He wanted to straighten her neck, but he couldn't bring himself to force her head in line with her body. He had a peculiar idea that he might hurt her. Pushing to his feet, he trudged over to the group standing near the wrecked engine. Maybe he could do some good here. Maybe involvement would ease his pain.

The cables strained as the colonel gave the signal to lift. The cables creaked and rattled as they slowly lifted the heavy engine into the air. Weatherall saw Tom Love and Jim Smith drop down by a broken Vic Lord, and he rushed forward to help them pull the crushed engineer from the wreckage. Vic's face was the color of lime. His eyes were dark holes of pain. The colonel reared up beside them and dropped to one knee. "You'll be all right, Vic."

Vic shook his head. "I'm a dead man. What about Steve?"

"He didn't have a chance. What happened?"

"I don't know. Everything just went crazy. One minute we were on the tracks; the next we were plowing up dirt. Tell Karen and the kids I loved them."

The colonel lurched to an erect position. He looked old. Tired. Beaten. "I've known that man for ten years. I know his wife. His family. What do I say to them? That he was killed building a damn railroad. Holy cow! Is it worth it?"

As two other men dragged out the dead fireman, Tom thumbed tobacco into his corncob. "You saying this wasn't an accident?"

Pain exploded across Weatherall's gut. His fist slammed into his open palm. "We're about to find out."

Tom glanced down at the two dead men. He fired his pipe. Jim wet his lips, his gaze fast on Weatherall. The colonel grunted, his features gray and grainy. Weatherall swung around the broken locomotive, with the others following. He led the way down track, to where the engine had jumped the line. They passed flipped flatcars, strewn metal, jumbled ties, their eyes following the rails. Tom said, "Look at that," and they saw where the right-hand rails had been disjointed. Tom fell to his knees. He wiggled a loose tie. "It was an accident. Somehow this tie broke loose. The engine just went off into space."

"You're positive it was an accident?" Weatherall said.

"Positive. This is loamy soil, Creed. Somebody was in a hurry. They didn't pack the dirt tight enough. That's the problem when you're trying to beat another line. You cut corners."

"Well, at least it wasn't murder," the colonel said.

Weatherall grunted. In a way, he wished it had been. At least he could have worked off some of his misery on others. He shook his head. Not a good thought for a man to hold. Charlotte would be ashamed of him. Thank God it was an accident. Enough people had been hurt already.

Nine o'clock in the evening found Weatherall brushing through the open flaps of Amos Bullard's Emporium. He knew he shouldn't be here, but he couldn't stand the quiet of his coach any longer. Perhaps in the midst of the noise and confusion here in the tents, he could forget his terrible loss for a few moments. He spotted Tom and Jim at a table and angled toward them. He didn't want to be alone. He needed company. His gaze locked on the bottle sitting atop their table. He'd already drunk a fifth, but it hadn't touched him. He'd drink more. He'd drink so much the world would be blotted out. He wished it could be blotted out forever.

Tom saw him, stood up. "Creed, sit down. Have a drink. Bartender, send another glass over here."

As Weatherall sank into a chair, someone thrust a glass before him. He stuck a cigar in his teeth, and Jim leaned over to hold a match to it. Jim's face was puffy and bruised, but his eyes were clear. If he'd suffered a mild concussion, he'd weathered it.

Weatherall gulped down his drink. He leaned back in his chair, puffed on the cigar. The place was packed. He studied the faces of the men filling the tent. He wondered how many of these men were like him — sitting here drinking, trying to dull the memory of a past gone wrong. Probably more than he'd ever suspected. When things were going right for you, you never thought they might be going wrong for someone else. Never thought — that was it. People weren't callous or indifferent. They were careless, and they were thoughtless. A man yelped back at the faro table. Talk ran high, and the band's tinny sound fluttered over the noisy rectangle. Someone pressed against the table, and

Weatherall glanced up to find Nelly May standing there.

"I'm sorry about your wife. I didn't know her, but everything I heard was good. I understand how you must feel."

A little pulse rose in Weatherall's cheek. How the hell could she understand? He started to say something, but her eyes stopped him. He saw sadness there, and he felt a sudden kinship with her. She did understand. It didn't make sense, but what he saw in her eyes mirrored the despair in his heart. He suddenly realized that this woman was deliberately letting him see beyond her tinseled front, and for a moment he forgot his own emptiness and recognized hers. He now realized he used to consider her nothing more than an object, an ornament, and he was reminded again of man's thoughtlessness.

His gaze shifted to young Smith, who looked up at Nelly May. What Jim felt for her was as plain as if it had been printed on his face. Weatherall glanced back at the blond saloon girl, but if she shared Jim's passion, it didn't show; caution suddenly shaded her eyes. Weatherall knew then that even if she cared for Jim she'd never admit it. She knew that what she was would follow her forever and if she loved Jim, she wouldn't strap that baggage to his back.

Nelly May smiled, "I'll be moving on. I'm a working girl."

"See you tomorrow night," Jim said as she moved away without acknowledging his comment.

The band swung out with "Alabama Gal" as Tom refilled the glasses. In the tent's rear, pool balls clicked, and a man said, "Good break." Some drunk at the bar broke into song, and tobacco smoke wreathed the air. Weatherall shifted around in his chair, trying to get comfortable. He was bone weary, but his only chance for sleep lay in the bottle on the table — plus two or three more like it. His mind shifted to Charlotte. She'd been smiling when she left that morning. Happy about the idea of putting in a day with men who loved and respected her. He could almost feel her body against his when she'd kissed him. Good God! That was only fifteen hours ago. How could he face the rest of his life without her!

Bullard's deep voice permeated Weatherall's withdrawal. "I'm sorry about your wife. She was a good woman. Not many of those to be found. Well, this night's on me. You boys order anything you want."

"He's right about one thing," Tom said. "Not many good women around. You were lucky to have one. Maybe that thought will ease you."

Weatherall nodded. He gulped his whiskey down, pulled the bottle toward him to refill the empty glass. He knew how everyone felt about Charlotte, and it was a comfort. But not enough comfort. He felt like a dead man. Nothing could touch him. Nothing, that was, but pain. He downed his whiskey, refilled his glass. There must be enough whiskey in this tent to shut off this mourning.

Tom reared back from the table, crossed his legs. "We made a good start cleaning up. We shouldn't lose more than a couple of days."

Weatherall nodded, trying to show interest he didn't feel. "I'd say we'll be in Canon City within a week."

"I've never been there," said Jim.

"Nice town. Got a hotel, stores, barbershop, even a mineral spring."

"Sounds great."

Tom said, "I guess that means the Denver line comes out ahead."

"Looks like it," Weatherall agreed. "Whoever gets into that gorge first wins the horseshoe match. There's no room for two railroads." He drew on his cigar, let smoke trickle from his nostrils, and downed half his drink. He didn't care about the railroad. He didn't care about anything. Still, he owed the colonel. He owed the crew. He'd stick it out, but when this line was finished, he'd move on. His entire life with Charlotte had been tied in with railroads. He couldn't do this kind of work anymore. Too many memories.

Dallas Mason walked up to the table. "I just got in from Pueblo. Heard the news. Creed, believe me, I had nothing to do with this."

"I know. Sit down. We'll drink to Charlotte."

"You know I don't drink."

"I said *sit* down."

"Sure. Sure. Let's have a drink."

Weatherall shouted for a glass, and after getting one poured four stiff shots. When he leaned back in his chair, he noted that Tom Love looked a bit uncomfortable, and Jim kept his eyes on the table. They both feared Dallas. They mistrusted him. He was on the other team. But Dallas had come in good faith. He'd come to comfort a friend. Weatherall lifted his glass. "Here's to the best woman who ever lived."

Glasses clinked. Tom said, "Amen," and they downed their whiskey. Three empty glasses hit the table, but Dallas's remained half full. "I'm sorry, Creed. I can't handle that much in one gulp." He leaned forward, his face close to Weatherall's. "What do you plan to do?"

"Finish the railroad."

"Why don't you move on? There's nothing here for you but unhappiness. Do your folks still own that spread outside Gila?"

"Yeah."

"Why don't you go there? Be with your family for a while."

"I can't walk out on the colonel."

"You have to think of yourself. Look in the mirror. You aren't any good to the colonel. You aren't any good to anybody. You hurt too much."

"I don't know what to do, Dallas."

"I know you don't. Creed, you're not even wearing your gun."

Weatherall's hand touched his hip. "I forgot."

"For a man with your job, that's a good way to get killed. It's all finished anyway."

"What do you mean?"

"I mean you're too far ahead of us. We aren't going to catch up."

"I don't know. I owe the colonel."

"Have it your way. I just wanted you to know I wasn't responsible for what happened."

As Dallas stood up, Weatherall nodded his thanks and watched Dallas stroll through the open flaps.

Tom refilled the glasses. "That man reminds me of a rattlesnake coiled behind a rock, waiting for somebody to walk by."

Weatherall's cigar had gone out, so he brought a match to it. No need to defend Dallas. He was like Nelly May. His reputation preceded him. No one would see, wanted to see, the good that was in him. Weatherall shook out his match. Dallas was right. After what had happened to Charlotte, he wasn't good for much. He wondered if he'd ever be again. Right now, it didn't seem to make much difference.

When Weatherall opened his eyes, darkness surrounded him. He lay there for a moment, not sure of his bearings, then realized he was lying on the horsehair settee in his living room. He stumbled to his feet and fired a match. Walking to the table, he lit the lamp and dropped his match into an ashtray. The inside of his mouth felt like it was full of fur, and his stomach was a queasy ball of melted lard. Somebody ran around inside his head beating a hammer, and his body screamed for water. He reeled over to the water bucket and downed three dippers in rapid succession. His thoughts went to the bedroom, where Charlotte was sleeping, and then reality hit him like a club. Charlotte wasn't in the bedroom. She'd never be in it again.

He fell into a chair as memory flooded him. He'd gone to Bullard's and got drunk with Jim and Tom. God only knew how or when he'd arrived home. Beyond Bullard's, he couldn't remember. He glanced out the pitch-black window. Nothing moved out there. It was too early. Charlotte! Charlotte dead. What would he do without her? Without realizing it, he stuck a cigar between his teeth and fired up. He felt sick. Everything reminded him of her. The curtains. The dried flowers. The slipcovers. She'd even painted the room. He took out his timepiece, saw it was five to four. The men wouldn't start moving for another hour. What was he going to do? How could he just sit here? His thoughts shot back to Sacramento. She'd been dressed in a man's pants and a man's heavy leather jacket. The pants had been formfitting, the jacket tight, and he'd felt a strong physical attraction the moment she walked into view. She hadn't glanced left or right, but the explosion of red hair framing her pale face and naturally pink lips had swung the attention of every man on that boarding block in her direction.

Later, on the train, after his run-in with Buck Weaton, they'd talked for a moment, and he'd brought her a cup of coffee. Her beauty had made him uncomfortable. He'd returned to the colonel's car with the distinct sensation that she didn't like him. But somehow they kept being thrown together. His discomfort had passed, as had her dislike; they'd become friends. He'd never considered falling in love with her. Not her. Not any woman. Not after how Aurora Wells had ripped him open. But love had happened. Sitting here now, he found it impossible to believe that Charlotte was gone forever. Then a picture of her pale face and oddly twisted neck filled his mind, bringing an agony so great he didn't believe he could bear it.

The door opened and Dallas Mason stepped inside the car. Startled, Weatherall half-rose, then sank back in his chair. "What are you doing here?"

Dallas's gaze swept the coach. He walked into the bedroom and returned carrying Weatherall's gunbelt and his Henry. "I'm taking over this railroad, Creed."

Weatherall's gaze didn't seem to focus. He squeezed his pounding forehead. "What are you talking about?"

"You've got a hangover. You're hurting. Now listen to me. I'm sending you and the colonel and your crew back to Denver. You're not making any more track."

Weatherall came to his feet. His thoughts suddenly cleared as a coldness gripped him. "So that's why you came to Bullard's. You wanted to see what kind of shape I was in."

"No. I wanted to tell you how sorry I was. To tell you I had nothing to do with that accident. Still, I could see you were in bad shape. That this was the time to move."

"I thought better of you, Dallas."

"Be reasonable. This way no one gets hurt. There's enough dead bodies already. Three of our men. Four or five of yours. Plus Charlotte. It isn't worth it."

"That's easy for you to say. But what about General Sheffield? The rest of the men who put up money for this line?"

"They can take the loss, but what about your loss? What about those two men crushed under that locomotive yesterday? Is money gonna replace them?"

Weatherall shook his head. He was drained. There was no fight left in him. What difference did it make? What difference did anything make?

"Pack your things. I'll treat your boys to a good breakfast, then send you on your way."

"Where's the colonel? The others?"

"They're being rousted out right now. This is for the best, Creed. You can go home. Spend some time with your folks. There can't be anything for you here now. Get your things together."

CHAPTER 12

Dimly aware of his surroundings, Weatherall slumped in his seat as the train clattered toward Pueblo. Across from him, Tom Love puffed on his corncob. Next to Tom, Jim Smith sat in sober silence, and to Weatherall's left, the colonel chewed on his cigar. This car, like the one ahead, was loaded with Denver hands; two Colorado men armed with shotguns guarded the coach, one stationed at the front end, one at the rear. The train had pulled out from camp about an hour ago, the miles clicking behind them. The Denver crew, settled in facing seats, were mostly silent. All were downcast about what had happened earlier this morning, when Dallas and his bunch had run them out of camp.

Weatherall glanced out at the flat, loamy plains. Grass greened the land, and scattered piñon and juniper formed the only breaks on the far-reaching prairie. Weatherall's gaze shifted to young Smith. Jim looked pale, and Weatherall knew he was thinking of Nelly May Scott. If Jim thought he hurt, he didn't understand what hurting was. Jim had only known Nelly May a few months, whereas Weatherall had been with Charlotte for three years. Weatherall's body seemed weighed down; a blackness closed over him. Nothing mattered anymore. Nothing.

Tom Love tapped out his burned-out corncob. "I guess this is the end of it."

"I'm afraid so," the colonel said.

"Mason sure outsmarted us."

"Give the devil his due. He knows his business."

Tom grunted, refilled his pipe. The colonel blew out a white streamer of smoke. Jim's gaze found Weatherall's, then shifted to the floor. In the back of the coach, someone snored softly. Weatherall felt exhausted himself. They'd had an early awakening, and they were all tired and discouraged. It was tough on any man to lose his job, particularly when he lost it without warning. And these men had given a lot to the railroad.

The colonel cleared his throat. "You know, Tom, I'm mad, madder than hell. Maybe I'll just hire a bunch of thugs when we reach Denver and retake the line."

Tom shook his head. "It's no good, Colonel. Mason would only hire more thugs and retake it. This railroad's cost enough. Check it off as a bad investment."

Weatherall glanced over at Tom. Something burned in Weatherall's chest, and — suddenly alert — he checked the guard at the front of the coach, then turned back to the man holding the rear. Those two seemed bored, inattentive. They stood with legs wide apart, shotguns hanging down at their sides. They didn't expect any trouble. Weatherall's thumb and forefinger squeezed his upper lip as rage shook him. Abruptly, he stood up, pushed into the aisle, and strolled toward the guard standing at the front door.

This fellow came erect. "Where do you think you're going?"

"Outside. Get some fresh air."

"You want fresh air, sit by the window."

When Weatherall continued his approach, the guard swung the shotgun waist high. "Did you hear me?"

At this point, Weatherall stood only five inches from the shotgun's muzzle. He halted, shrugged. "I don't want no trouble." But as he wheeled left, his hand shot out to grab the scattergun and thrust the muzzle skyward. One barrel exploded with a blast that rocked the coach, and pieces of debris fell on Weatherall's head and shoulders from the hole ripped through the roof. Continuing his turn, Weatherall slammed a down-driving right into the guard's chin. When Weatherall's fist hit bone, the guard's knees buckled like a newborn calf's. As the fellow sagged, Weatherall grabbed the shotgun with one hand, the man's shirt collar with the other hand, and whirled so that the guard formed a shield between Weatherall and the Colorado hand at the far end of the coach. Weatherall pointed both barrels at the man down the aisle, who had brought his shotgun to a shooting position. "Your friend gets the full load, not me. I suggest you drop it."

The Colorado tough's eyes rounded. He wet his lips uncertainly. Suddenly Sam White rocketed out of the seat to the guard's right. He drove his huge frame into the man's shoulder, knocking him into the laps of Will Johnson and Jack Brown. Johnson and Brown wrestled the gun from the man's loose fingers, then threw him to the floor and pinned him there.

Weatherall released the man who had been his shield and whirled to face the door. He heard the thump as the man he'd held hit the floor, and then the door flew open before a Colorado hired gun carrying a raised shotgun. Weatherall kept his weapon waist high. He said, "It's a no-win game. Is the railroad worth that much to you?"

The Colorado roughneck shook his head. He handed his gun to George Duncan, who occupied the seat next to the aisle. Duncan stood up, pushed the stolid-faced guard into a seat, then looked at Weatherall. "What now?"

"Keep your eye on him. There's one last man in the other car." Weatherall swung around Duncan, stepped through the door onto the platform, and crossed to the front car. He hammered on the front door, "You in there. We'll turn you loose at Pueblo. My word on it."

"You Creed Weatherall?"

"That's right."

Silence came from the coach. The wheels clacked against the track. Wind threatened to whip Weatherall's hat off.

The fellow inside said, "All right, I'm coming out," and seconds later shoved through the door to hand Weatherall his shotgun and gunbelt.

Back in the rear coach, Weatherall handed the gunbelt to Randy Roberts. "Go over the top and take the engine. Slow it to a crawl and hold it there for ten minutes, then highball it for Pueblo." As Randy started forward, Creed clipped down the aisle to where the colonel had risen from his seat. "Colonel, I'm taking back this railroad. In Pueblo, I want you to arm every man on this train, then head back for camp. I'll expect you by noon tomorrow."

Tom leaped to his feet, threw a fist in the air, and yelled "Yippee!" Jim echoed that yell as men shouted up and down the coach. Lee Keene rushed forward to shake Weatherall's hand, and the colonel smothered Weatherall in a bear hug. The colonel stepped back. "What do you intend to do?"

"Catch them by surprise the way they did us. Jim, I want you, Tom, Sam, George, and Lee to come with me. Now I'm volunteering you, but how about it?"

A chorus of "We're with you!" rang out, and the men named gathered around Weatherall. The colonel stepped forward, expelled a cloud of cigar smoke. "What happened? You said we couldn't fight Mason."

"I was wrong. We have to fight him."

"But why?

Weatherall shrugged and left it at that, but he knew why. When Tom Love had said to check this off as a bad investment, Weatherall had known that couldn't be right. He couldn't live with the thought that Charlotte had died for nothing, and it wasn't fair to the families of others who'd been killed. Every mile of this track was covered with blood. It couldn't be for nothing. He owed Charlotte and those men too much.

Wheels screeched. The coach's swaying slackened. Weatherall turned to his crew.

"We'll drop off here."

"But Creed," Tom said, "on this prairie we can be spotted for miles. We'll stand out like elephants."

"We'll lay in by the river until dark. Then we'll move in. We'll take back the camp tomorrow morning, after the work crew has pulled out. Shouldn't be too many people left behind. If we can get by Dallas Mason, we're home free."

"And if we don't get by him?"

"Your guess is as good as mine."

The hands of Weatherall's American Horologe pointed to seven when the work train pulled out of the Colorado's new main camp. Weatherall and his men had worked their way to within a hundred yards of the camp; they lay in a buffalo wallow paralleling the river. Early-morning sunlight freshened the plains, and piñons scented the air. Weatherall held his place, knowing he couldn't move until he spotted the exact location of Dallas Mason. The Colorado's lone gunhand had accompanied the train, and four men had hiked toward the corral and maintenance area. That left the cooks in the mess tent, but Dallas was the key, and he hadn't been seen yet.

Weatherall rolled over on his side, studied the six individuals packed into the wallow

239

beside him. They looked wary but determined. Weatherall rolled back to the front. He needed a cup of coffee. A smoke. He was bone weary. His thoughts centered on Charlotte, and sadness filtered into every cranny of his being. He still found it impossible to realize that she was dead. Since their marriage, they'd always been together. After they'd shared their honeymoon in Denver, they'd spent two weeks in Gila Bend with his folks. They'd loved Charlotte. But then, everyone had loved Charlotte.

Weatherall's gaze settled on a short, squatty individual, dressed in white ducks and a brown coat, emerging from the mess tent. A second man stepped into view, and Weatherall's heart jumped. That man was Dallas Mason, so the short fellow, whom Weatherall had never seen, had to be Don Adams, head of the Colorado line. It hadn't taken him long to move in. Weatherall watched the two of them until they reached the colonel's coach and disappeared inside.

He glanced at the men grouped around him. "Sam, you and George take out the compound. Tom, you and Lee take the mess hall. Jim, you and I will take the coach."

As the others moved out, Weatherall and Jim headed for the coach. The morning was so still that one would have thought the camp was empty. Weatherall and Jim quick-stepped to the coach, and with his shotgun leveled gut high, Weatherall shouldered inside, with Jim close behind.

The short, squat Adams sat at the end of the table facing the doorway. At Weatherall's entrance his pie face reflected surprise that was immediately replaced with malice. Dallas sat next to his boss, and he followed Adams's gaze to the doorway. "I didn't expect to see you."

"I was counting on that."

Adams fingered his brown beard. Anger burned his cheeks. "Well, Dallas, it seems you were wrong again. So this is the famous Creed Weatherall."

"You guessed it."

"And just what do you have in mind?"

"Taking back this railroad."

"That might not be as easy as you think."

"It won't be that difficult. Your crew won't be back until dark. Mine will be here at noon. Dallas, from here out all Denver men will be armed. I'll have guards out twenty-four hours a day carrying scatterguns. There won't be any more surprises."

Adams played with his watch chain. His eyes turned cold as frost, and anger thinned his meaty lips. "You want trouble, I can give you trouble."

Weatherall shifted so that his shotgun pointed directly at the smoldering Colorado owner. Weatherall had never met Adams until now, but he instinctively disliked the man. Adams was arrogant, high-handed, obviously used to getting his own way. He considered this an unnecessary setback, but he wasn't about to quit. Weatherall grunted. "You can have it any way you want it. I intend to see that this line gets through."

Adams stood up. He tried to look taller than his five feet six inches. "You know, a man with your attitude could get killed."

"So could a man with yours. Now pack up and head back across the river."

Adams bared his teeth. His face turned a caboose red, and his back stiffened into a railroad spike. Without a word, he swung around Dallas and stepped out of the coach. Dallas got to his feet. "Nice to see somebody put that little bastard in his place."

"If you dislike him so much, why do you work for him?"

"Money. Be seeing you," Dallas said, and strolled from the coach.

Weatherall released a long breath, then heeled around to Jim Smith, whose strained features relaxed. "Everything went so easy. It worked out just like you planned."

"The game's not over yet. We've got to

try and figure out what Adams will plan next."

"What do we do now?"

"I'm going to see that Adams and his crew get across the river. I suggest that you go see Nelly May."

Jim's lips worked strangely. Uncertainty hollowed his eyes. "Why?"

"Because you're busting a gut wanting to."

"I don't know, Creed. Maybe you were right."

"Maybe I was. Maybe I wasn't. All I know is that without love, life isn't worth living. If that girl wants you, marry her and get her out of that tent."

Nelly May Scott seemed to hear a voice somewhere in the distance. The voice grew louder, and as her eyes slowly opened, she realized the voice came from just outside the tent. As she struggled up on one elbow, her gaze fell on the clock. What idiot would be waking her at this hour? Someone shouted again, and her heart gave a funny jump when she recognized Jim's voice. She said, "I'm coming," sprang to her feet, and dashed to the tent flap without even pausing to put on her slippers or peignoir. She pushed open the flap to stare into Jim's eager face. "Jim! What's wrong? You're supposed to be in Pueblo."

He grabbed both her shoulders. "Nothing's wrong. We took the camp back. Booted Adams across the river."

"My God! Anybody hurt?"

"Not a shot fired."

"What are you doing here?"

"I wanted to see you."

"Well, couldn't it wait until tonight? It's only eight-thirty. I need my sleep."

"That's why I'm here. I mean to change that."

"What are you talking about?"

"I want to marry you."

Her mouth lost its shape, and she stared at him as if he were a gibbering idiot. "Are you drunk?"

"No. Just in love."

She stared fixedly and incredulously as her heart rattled around in her chest like dice in a leather cup. That he loved her. That he would ask her to marry him. Her of all people. "You're talking nonsense."

"Do you love me?"

"Jim, I've been a prostitute since I was fourteen years old."

"I don't care. Do you love me?"

A chill ran through her body. She was afraid to speak. Of course she loved him. But what he asked was out of the question. She was nothing but a common whore. Society would never let her be anything else.

He took her hands. His blue eyes pleaded. "You do love me. I know you do."

She felt giddy, weak. She studied his bronze, handsome face. The way his yellow hair fell over his forehead. His quick, easy smile broke his lips, and her heart fluttered like a wounded bird. Good God! How she wanted this man and all he promised. But it was too late. "Jim, do you know what you're saying?"

"I know."

Desperation coiled in the pit of her stomach. She didn't want to hurt him. But hurting him now was better than hurting him for the rest of his life. "I don't know if I love you or not. What does the word mean?"

Jim shrugged. He fumbled for words. "Love's hard to define. It's a feeling."

"I've heard that before . . ."

"Look. I don't know. I guess it's when you always want to be with someone. When you're not happy away from her."

"Do you want to be with me?"

"Yes."

"That's exactly what Brett said. However, it didn't take long for that feeling to wear off. About six months, as a matter of fact."

"All I want to know is if you love me or not."

"It doesn't make any difference. There's

no chance for us."

"I think you answered my question."

She shook her head. She felt trapped. Desperate. Why couldn't he see the line drawn between them? "I think you should leave. This is foolish. Why did you come here?"

"Creed Weatherall told me to."

"Creed Weatherall! He thinks I'm right for you?"

"All I know is that he said that life without love wasn't worth living."

She couldn't get her breath. She wheeled back into the tent so that he couldn't see her tears. She was a fool. Jim was a fool. And Creed Weatherall was the biggest fool of all. He should never have sent Jim here. She would ruin his life. She sank down on the side of her bed, wiped her eyes. God! What a mess. A painful mess.

Jim had followed her inside and stood humbly next to her bed. Her heart was breaking. She wanted to reach out and draw him to her, but common sense told her to drive him away. He had too much to offer. Too much to give. He couldn't be tied to a woman like her. "Jim, have you ever been in love?"

"No."

"Neither have I, but I thought I was. Let me ask you a question. Have you ever wanted to go to bed with me?"

He blushed. "Yes."

"Then why haven't you?"

"I don't know. It just didn't seem right. But I wanted to."

"Jim, what you call love is infatuation. Lust. Not love."

"I didn't fight Tully Williams for lust."

"You just don't think you did. You're young. Inexperienced. You're confused."

"I may be young, but I know what love is."

She shook her head. She'd never encountered anything like this. She didn't know how to handle it. Maybe he did love her. She certainly loved him, but none of that mattered. Only Jim's future mattered. He had to pursue his dreams, and he couldn't do that with her at his side. She released a long, heavy sigh, wiped at her eyes. "Jim, how do you know what love is?"

"You just know. Take my mother and father. They loved each other."

"But how do you know? Did they ever say so?"

"Not to my recollection."

"Then how do you know?"

"I just know."

"Did you have any other family?"

"Two sisters and two brothers."

"Maybe your mother and father stayed

together because of them."

"I told you I couldn't define it, but I can give you an example right here in this camp."

"This hellhole? I don't believe it."

"Did you ever see Charlotte and Creed Weatherall look at each other?"

Nelly May's heart seemed to fill her chest. She caught her breath. A picture of Weatherall's rugged countenance flashed before her — the day he'd arrived in camp bringing the broken remains of his wife. No one could have mistaken the despair, the misery stamped on his lifeless face. He'd looked as dead as the woman he'd cradled in his arms. And Nelly May had seen something else. Fear had shadowed Weatherall's eyes, flattened his bronzed cheeks. She'd understood, because deep inside she buried that same fear. She kept it layered with cynicism, so that she could deny its existence. But it was there. The fear of being alone. When she looked up at Jim's earnest features, she almost broke. Then she pushed her feelings behind years of calculated reserve.

Jim touched her shoulder. "You know, don't you?"

She tried to look away. Tried to fight back the feelings that battered her reserve. She couldn't know. She didn't want to know. She didn't want Jim to get caught in this emotional cross fire. He would be hurt, as Creed Weatherall had been hurt. Her love could only destroy him.

"Why do you fight it? You know you love me."

She tried to laugh, but her lips only trembled. Emotions surged in her breast. Emotions that she had long repressed. She felt light-headed, yet strangely at peace. "What do you want me to do?"

"Three or four days from now, I go to Denver for supplies. I want you to go with me. We'll be married there."

Unable to speak, she nodded. Suddenly, her head was buried in his chest, and she was wiping away tears that blinded her. His arms held her fast, and she clung to him as if afraid he would get away. This would work. It had to work. If anything happened to tear them apart, she couldn't go on. Creed Weatherall was right. Life without love wasn't worth living.

CHAPTER 13

Colonel Wade Thompson soaked the butt of his cigar in his bourbon glass, then leaned back contentedly in his chair. He sat at a table in the center of Bullard's tent which he occupied with Weatherall, Jim Smith, and Nelly May Scott. The tent was filled to capacity with railroaders from both the Denver and Colorado lines. The colonel stared at Weatherall, who puffed on a cigar. "We're moving right along. Be in Canon City in a few days."

"Looks like it," Weatherall responded.

The colonel chewed on his cigar. He studied Weatherall, noting the big man's indifferent expression. Weatherall had never been much of a talker, but since Charlotte's death he had pulled inward. That was the reason for this party. The colonel had said that it was to celebrate Jim and Nelly May's upcoming wedding, but the real purpose was to get Weatherall moving. He didn't need to think. He needed to stay busy. The colonel glanced around the tent, fighting his own sadness. Weatherall seemed like a son to him, and

Charlotte had been like a daughter. He hurt too, so he could imagine how Weatherall felt.

At least Jim and Nelly May were happy, but the colonel was concerned. Jim had a future before him, and Nelly May — well, she had a background. He glanced down the bar, spotting familiar faces. Tom Love downed a boilermaker while Sam White swigged a bottle of tequila. The colonel couldn't understand anyone drinking tequila. The stuff tasted like a mouthful of mush. He swung back to the table, lifted his glass. "Here's to the married-couple-to-be. A long and happy life."

Weatherall hoisted his glass. "I'll drink to that."

A smile flashed across young Smith's face, and Nelly May blushed. The colonel set his glass on the table, puffed on his cigar. "We're going to miss you around here, Jim."

"What are you talking about?"

"I don't think a newly married man will want to be separated from his bride."

"Creed said Nelly May and I could have his place."

"It won't work, son. I made one exception for Creed, but it's not fair to the other married men to make another. That kind of thing causes resentment."

"But, Colonel, I don't want to leave the railroad."

The colonel noted that Nelly May had lowered her head. She seemed resigned. He didn't want to hurt either one of them, but they'd be better off somewhere else. The men in this camp could never forget what Nelly May had been, and with her beauty, she'd be a constant target for remarks that Jim would have to stop.

Weatherall reached for the bottle, refilled his glass. "The colonel's right, Jim. I wasn't thinking."

"But this is my job!"

The colonel put both hands on his knees. "You've got a new job. When you ship those supplies from Denver, head for San Francisco. I've wired my foreman, Wade Meek. He's expecting you. He'll help you get your surveying license, and then I want you to take over the office."

Jim's jaw dropped a foot. "But, Colonel, how's Wade going to take this?"

"He's getting old, like me. He'll be glad to have some new blood in the place. Now, of course, if you'd prefer to go out on your own . . ."

Jim looked at Nelly May, who looked at the colonel. Jim wet his lips excitedly. "Why are you doing this? I mean it's too much."

"Not really. You know June and I only had one boy, Thomas. Diphtheria killed him when he was two years old. After that, June couldn't have any more children, so since she died ten years ago, I've been alone. Then I met you and Creed. You two kinda became my family. This way I can keep you close, but you can do what you want to do."

Weatherall leaned forward. "Colonel, that was a nice thing to say."

Nelly May put her hand on the colonel's arm. "That was a beautiful thing to say. I hope someday you'll include me in your family."

Jim tried to speak, but settled for a long draw on his cigar, and the colonel nodded. They were his family. The colonel was pleased to know they felt something for him, too. As for Nelly May, eventually he might feel close to her. That was up to her.

The colonel glanced up to see Dallas Mason angle through the front flap. Dallas paused, surveyed the tent. He found their table, and weary acceptance marked his face. He pushed over to their table and stood facing Weatherall. The colonel sensed something was wrong here. Terribly wrong. The room grew quiet and the colonel felt a sudden chill.

Weatherall glanced up. "Dallas, good to see you. Sit down and join the party."

The colonel chewed on his cigar. That Weatherall didn't notice the change proved how deeply involved he was in his loss. The colonel watched as Dallas fingered the old bullet wound puckering his cheek.

Dallas stared down at Weatherall, glanced away, then looked back with stolid determination. "Creed, you're going to have to leave camp."

"What are you talking about?"

"Look, it's my job to stop this railroad. I can't do that with you here. You've got to leave. I want you to saddle up and ride out in the morning. I want your word on it."

"Dallas, I can't do that."

"Damn it! You've got to do it. Don't you understand? If you don't go, I've got to call you out."

"So it's come to that."

"Do you think I want this? Listen to me. This railroad doesn't mean a damn thing to you. Ride out. You're not a gunfighter. No one's going to blame you for ducking a shoot-out with Dallas Mason."

"Dallas, I can't go."

"Creed, I'm begging you."

Weatherall shook his head. "I'm sorry."

"Damn it, man. Don't make me kill you."

"Dallas, I've got a job to do."

"Your job doesn't involve facing me. The colonel doesn't expect that. Ask him."

"What the colonel thinks changes nothing. I have my own reasons. This line is going through."

Dallas let out a long breath. His hands rolled into fists, opened, formed fists again. He stood there, opening and closing his hands into fists, a long time. "Tomorrow morning then. At sunrise, out there on the street." His face blanched white as fresh paint, Dallas whirled and marched straight-backed out of the tent.

In the tent not one man moved. Not one man spoke. Then someone tipped a glass over at the bar, muttered, "Son of a bitch," and the room burst into forced gaiety. Men and saloon women chattered too loudly. The band swung into an off-key waltz as the roulette wheel started its incessant clatter.

The colonel said, "Creed, tomorrow morning you saddle up and ride out. You can't face Mason."

"No dice, Colonel."

"You don't understand. You no longer work for the railroad."

"It's no good, Colonel. This is something I have to do."

"Holy cow! We're only two days from Canon City. The men are well armed. Mason can't stop us now."

"Colonel, without me, these men can't face Dallas. You know it and I know it."

"I don't care. I'm ordering you to leave."

Jim leaned forward, his face sly and eager. "After midnight, we can get the boys together.

Hit the Colorado camp. We'll run the whole gang out of the country. I'll kill Dallas myself. Blow his head off with a shotgun."

Weatherall shook his head. "Thanks, Jim, but you don't know what you're saying. All that will accomplish is killing a bunch of good men on both sides."

The cigar fell apart in the colonel's mouth, and he flung it to the dirt floor. "I can't understand why you're doing this."

Nelly May's lips tightened. Her eyes narrowed as she brought her hands together. "You have to do it because of Charlotte, don't you?"

Weatherall's lips crooked in a sad smile. "Jim, you have a very perceptive young lady. I think she'll be good for you."

Jim's features hardened. "I still think I ought to take a shotgun to him."

"That would be murder."

"He's not above murdering you."

"Dallas is doing what he has to do."

The colonel snorted, slammed his fist into his open palm. "Why do you always defend that killer? You've always said he'd never draw on you. Why not?"

"He owes me. I saved his life."

"That was a mistake. What are you going to do?"

"Right now, go over to the coach. Charlotte

carried a thirty-two when she worked the tables. I'm going to be sure it's in working order for tomorrow."

The colonel sagged back in his chair. His arms dropped to his sides. "A thirty-two! Holy cow. Are you crazy? You need all the firepower you can get."

Weatherall got to his feet and looked down at the three of them. "Sorry to spoil the party," he said and, turning, walked away.

The colonel's gaze followed Weatherall's back until it disappeared through the tent flap. Then he lit a fresh cigar and stared at the table. Around him men talked. They admired Creed Weatherall. They didn't like what was about to happen. The colonel glanced at Jim, who unconsciously fingered his shirt buttons. His face was drawn. Worried. Next to him, Nelly May turned her glass around and around on the table. She didn't know Creed as well as the others did, but she knew him well enough to understand what kind of a man he was.

The colonel reached for the bourbon bottle and filled his glass to the rim. "I'm going to get drunk. Anyone care to join me?"

Nelly May glanced up from the table. "I've never been drunk."

"Then this is a good time to start. You'll feel so bad in the morning that what happens won't hurt so much."

Jim pulled the bottle toward him. "You stay sober, Nelly May. Somebody has to see that the colonel and I get home."

Daybreak's thin shadows threw irregular patterns over the land. The heavy odor of black coffee still filled Weatherall's nostrils as he stepped from the mess hall and gazed across the tracks toward the town. Front Street was loaded with railroaders and townspeople. He had had little sleep last night. At the end of the street, about a hundred yards distant, Bullard's Emporium was agleam with lamplight. Weatherall could make out Dallas's big-shouldered form in front of the tent. Next to him stood the squat, potbellied Don Adams; he looked up at Dallas and said something, but Dallas held up a hand to quiet him when Weatherall moved out of the mess tent's shadows.

Men from the Colorado line piled around the street's southern end; the street was lined with hell-on-wheels townspeople. Most of them were here for the excitement. They didn't care who died. The town won either way. The games, the muggings, the cheating, the prostitution would continue. At the street's north end, the Denver crew huddled quietly except for some casual whispering, and even that ceased when Weatherall crossed the tracks and stood facing Dallas, who waited at the street's far end. Even at this distance, Dallas's angular face was easy to recognize, and Weatherall thought he read weary resignation in it. He felt the same way himself.

The colonel broke through the crowd, stepped to Weatherall's side. He put a hand on Weatherall's shoulder. "Son, you don't have to do this."

Weatherall looked at the colonel for the first time. The man's eyes were red from drink and lack of sleep. His shoulders sagged in gray defeat. His shoulders suddenly drooped, and he rounded back to the group of Denver people standing near the head of the street. Weatherall considered those individuals. He'd known some of them for four years. They went back to his first railroad job, with the Central Pacific. Sam White and Lee Keene met his gaze, but for the most part the others avoided it. He saw George Duncan, Ace Benson, Joe Yates, Tom Love — all the men he'd worked with. They'd gathered here to support him the only way they could. He also saw Jim Smith and Nelly May. He wished she weren't here. What was about to happen wouldn't be pretty. But, he supposed, with her background, she'd seen it all. For some idiotic reason, he hoped it mattered this time.

The sun formed a quarter-circle above the horizon. The wind carried a sweet fragrance. A magpie chattered from a juniper stand beyond the river, while a pale mist swirled along the banks. The sky glowed with yellows, pinks, and reds against a blue background. It was going to be a beautiful day. Suddenly, for the first time since Charlotte had died, Weatherall wanted to live. He wanted to grow beyond his pain, to find the peace that time would bring. He owed it to Charlotte. He owed it to himself.

He saw Adams edge away from Dallas, who moved forward with slow, measured steps. Weatherall moistened his lips. Sweat beaded the small of his back. His stomach was an empty, hollow place. When he stepped forward, the slight murmuring that had sounded behind him ceased as an absolute silence descended over the street. Weatherall passed the R and R Hotel; he saw Cal Reed on the porch, but Cal's wife, Norma, was nowhere in sight. Weatherall hoofed past the barbershop, past Trueheart's Saloon. As his eyes focused on Dallas, the people lining both sides of the street formed a blur. Abruptly, Weatherall halted. About fifty yards separated the two men, and Weatherall reached for the thirty-two tucked in his waistband. As his fingers closed over its handle, Dallas's first shot boomed over the camp, but it was wide. Weatherall straightened his arm, sighted, eased back the hammer as Dallas's second slug tunneled through empty air. Dallas's third shot wickedly whistled by Weatherall's ear as Weatherall squeezed the trigger. He saw Dallas's arm sag, heard a sharp report; the handgun bucked against his palm.

Relief melted the tension constricting Weatherall's back as Dallas's gun fell free from his hand. Weatherall saw pain crease Dallas's cheeks; then Dallas dropped to his knees and fumbled for his revolver with his left hand. With complete detachment, Weatherall squeezed off a second round, which buried itself in Dallas's left shoulder. Dallas's head lowered, and he balanced there on both knees, staring at the dirt.

Cheers rang out from the Denver gang, while the Colorado bunch stood in disbelief. Someone in the crowd fired a pistol in the air, and a dog barked excitedly. Down street, Adams's reddish complexion turned a pasty white, and after throwing Weatherall a hard look he faded into the men behind him. The Denver crew surrounded Weatherall. They laughed, shouted, pounded him on the back. The colonel hugged him, and Tom Love shook his hand.

Weatherall shouldered through the surrounding men to walk down to where Dallas knelt in the street.

Dallas didn't look up. "Why didn't you just kill me?"

"I didn't want to have to live with that."

"How did you know?"

"An educated guess. You're getting older, and sunrise is a strange time to call a man out. It all added up. You wanted me up close so you could see me."

"I guess this finishes it."

"I guess it does." Weatherall swung back to the men crowding around him, searched until he found Doc Prichard's shriveled countenance. "Take him to the hospital and dig out the lead. Patch him up." As Doc and Sam helped Dallas to his feet, Weatherall's gaze settled on Will Johnson. "Time to take them out, Will. We've got to make track."

Will grinned. He nodded eagerly. "Come on, boys. We've a day ahead of us. I mean to break a record."

"Sounds like eleven miles," said Weatherall.

"Eleven it is. See you about dark."

As the men hustled toward the work train, Weatherall lit a cigar with a shaking match. The tobacco stung his mouth, his throat, his nostrils. It reaffirmed that he was still alive. The colonel puffed on his own cigar. "What if you'd figured this wrong?"

"Wouldn't have made any difference. I couldn't outdraw him anyway."

"I guess we can drive the line on through now."

"Right. Adams hasn't got time to regroup. You'll be in Canon City tomorrow night. Let's get some breakfast. All of a sudden, I'm hungry."

As they sauntered up the street, Weatherall saw Jim Smith's yellow hair among the departing work crew. Nelly May swung off to the coach. They seemed to truly care for one another. He had a hunch that things were going to work out for them. He glanced down at his companion. "Colonel, one thing Dallas said was right. I need to get away. Too many memories. Every where I look I see Charlotte. I think I'll go home, work some cattle, mend some fences, bale some hay. Maybe after a while, I'll be able to handle this. Right now I can't."

The colonel nodded. "Take as much time as you need. You know how to get in touch with me. One good thing about memories, Creed. Over the years, we tend to hold on to the good ones and forget the bad."

Weatherall grunted. That was what he hoped for. It was the only thing that kept him going. He never wanted to forget Charlotte, what they'd shared, but he wanted to lose this pain. Someday, he'd be back with the colonel. Someday, they'd build another railroad. But for now he wanted to find peace. The aroma of fresh coffee hit him as they entered the mess tent. It smelled good. He knew it was a harbinger of the future.